CHANCE

COPYRIGHT

First Original Edition, April 2015
Copyright © 2015 by Deborah Bladon
ISBN: 9781926440248
Cover Design by Wolf & Eagle Media

This book is a work of fiction. Any resemblance to actual persons, living or dead, or actual events is entirely coincidental. Names, characters, businesses, organizations, places, events and situations either are the product of the author's imagination or are used factiously.
All rights reserved. No parts of this book may be reproduced in any form or by any means without written consent from the author.

ISBN: 1512063207
ISBN-13: 9781512063202

CHANCE

A Novel

New York Times & USA Today Bestselling Author
DEBORAH BLADON

Also by Deborah Bladon
The Obsessed Series
The Exposed Series
The Pulse Series
The Vain Series
The Ruin Series
Impulse
Solo
The Gone Series
Fuse
The Trace Series

ONE

"You're telling me that I've never fucked you?"

You'd think I'd walk away at this point. It would make sense for me to turn on my heel and march out of his apartment. I'm not even sure why I'm here.

Today started out like any other day. I woke up and then I had a glass of orange juice after I brushed my teeth. I cursed myself for doing that and vowed that tomorrow I'd drink the orange juice before I brushed my teeth. I dressed in a navy blue pencil skirt and a pale blue blouse. I'd let my dark brown hair fall in waves down my back and I'd hurried to make the subway train before it sped uptown. I walked through the door of my office at precisely two minutes before nine. It was the same routine I followed every single day.

I spent my morning in meetings with the development team and I had lunch with the owner of the company. He'd been focused on his phone. It's normal for him. He can't resist his wife and whenever she texts or calls him, the world, as he knows it, halts on its axis.

Once I got back to my office, I settled in at my desk to go over last month's budget. It was exactly five minutes to two when my phone rang and I dropped everything to get in a taxi to come here. I'm in a spacious apartment on Park Avenue, sitting across from the one man who has popped in and out of my life since I was a child.

"Caleb," I say his name as I cross my arms over my chest. "What the hell was the emergency? Why am I even here?"

His finger darts into the air to silence me. It's a gesture that he knows I can't stand. He's pushing me and if I thought it would benefit me at all, I'd push him right back. I know his game though. I know exactly what's going on.

"I have to go." His deep voice fills the room. "I'll call you later, baby."

I shake my head slightly as he ends the call. "If you called me down here so I could listen to you talk to some woman who can't remember being fucked by you, I have better things to do with my time."

"I didn't fuck her." He pushes his chair back from the desk as he crosses his long legs. "If I had, she'd remember it."

I cover my face with my hands. "I have a lot to do today. I have to get back to my office."

"Why haven't you quit that job yet, Rowan?" His hand darts into the air. "I need you to work with me. I'm prepared to sweeten the offer."

"What offer?" I fumble inside my purse for my smartphone. "You know I'm never going to work for you."

"I know that you will one day." He stands quickly, pulling his large frame up. "Tell me what they're paying you at Corteck and I'll double it."

"I'm not telling you how much money I make." I scan my phone, reading the new emails that have come in since I left the office almost an hour ago. "When have I ever told you how much money I make?"

"When you worked at that fast food place right before you graduated from high school," he points out. "I told you my professor assigned a project about young people in the workplace and you let me interview you."

"You were such an asshole." I don't look up from my phone. "You were twenty-two, Caleb. You should have been partying hard. Instead you were harassing me."

"I was curious." He rounds the desk. "I wanted you to come and work for me then, don't you remember?"

I do remember. I remember how envious I was that he was able to work for his father and that he was pulling in more money than my parents were making combined. Caleb Foster has never had to do an honest day's work in his life and he's still trying to get me to pick up the slack for him.

"I like my job at Corteck. I work in a real office." I scan the home office we're standing in. "Don't you ever actually go into the office building that has your last name plastered all over the front of it?"

"You mean that one you pass every day when you go to your job at Corteck?"

"I need to leave," I say briskly. "Don't keep calling me down here for nothing. I have a job to do."

"One day you're going to ditch all that so you can work with me." He grabs my arm as I walk past him.

I stare up into his face. His body may have changed since we were children but the same glint in his dark eyes that I saw when he chased me around the playground is still there. His short hair is a darker shade of brown now than it used to be. There's no denying that he's gorgeous. He knows it and he uses it at every opportunity. He's tall and muscular and if I didn't know him as well as I do, I might even label him as emotionally dangerous. It's the reason I've always avoided getting romantically entangled with him. Caleb breaks hearts whether he's aware of it or not.

"I'm leaving." I pull my arm free of his grasp. "Don't call me again unless you actually need something from me. I'm tired of you wasting my time."

'You don't mean that Rowan." He moves in step beside me. "You don't actually mean that you'd rather I don't call you."

"I mean exactly that." I pat him on the chest. "You can't just interrupt my life for your bullshit."

He presses the call button for the elevator. "It's not bullshit. I'm hurt that you think that's what it is."

I sense the grin on his handsome face before I see it. "Why am I even here? You could have offered me the job on the phone."

"You always say no when I ask you on the phone."

"That's because I'm never going to work for you." I push the call button again. "Is the elevator broken again?"

"It looks that way." He gestures towards a door a few feet from us. "You can take the stairs or you can wait until they fix it."

"I have a lot to do today. I can do the stairs."

I follow him through the doorway into a long and narrow hallway. "Do you want me to walk down with you?" He raises a brow.

"I'll be fine." I reach to open the door to the stairway but it doesn't budge. "Is this broken too? You'd think a building on Park Avenue would have a better maintenance man."

"The door is fine." He grabs hold of the door handle and gives it a quick twist. He swings it open effortlessly. "You're sure you don't want me to walk down with you?"

"Of course not." I brush past him into the stairwell. "Promise me you're not going to keep calling me for nothing. I have important things going on in my life right now."

"More important than me?" He swings his arms in the air as he walks into the small space. "Don't try and tell me that our friendship doesn't mean everything to you, Rowan."

"It doesn't." I laugh as I look up at him. "You know that it doesn't."

"You've broken my heart." He pulls both hands to his chest as he takes a heavy step back. "You can hear it breaking, can't you?"

I turn towards the concrete stairs. "I came here for nothing. I need to get back to work."

"Wait." He tugs lightly on the side of my skirt. "There is something I need to tell you."

I roll my eyes. "Why do you insist on wasting my time? It's just a game to you. You're lucky my boss doesn't care when I leave in the middle of the day."

"This isn't a game." He swallows hard. "I do need to tell you something. I have to tell you something. I just don't know how to."

I've known Caleb Foster my entire life. I know the instant when something is wrong. A sudden darkness has overtaken his face. It's not just the lighting in this dim and musty stairwell.

"Row." His jaw tightens. "I'm sorry, Rowan. I can't believe I have to tell you this."

"Tell me what?" I grab onto the lapel of his suit jacket. "Just tell me. You're scaring me now."

His hands clench at his sides. His lips move faintly but nothing comes out.

"Caleb, tell me."

He cups his fingers around my chin and looks directly into my eyes. "Promise me you'll still be my friend when I tell you. Promise me you won't stop talking to me."

"I promise," I whisper softly. "I'll always be your friend."

"You're the only person I can tell this to. You're the only person who'll understand," he starts before he pauses to draw in a deep breath.

I feel my face heating. I know that the words that he's about to say to me are going to impact me deeply. I see it in his expression and I feel it in his touch. I don't like being this close to him. I've learned skillfully how to avoid being alone with him. He makes me feel things I don't want to acknowledge. I may be able to convince him that he's just a good friend when we're sitting in a room filled with others, or when there's a desk between us. When we're like this, alone, without the welcome barrier of other people or things, I feel vulnerable and exposed.

I lick my bottom lip. I want to say something that will coax the truth out of him. The tone of his voice gave absolutely nothing away when he called me earlier. He didn't sound panicked. There was no urgency woven into his words. He simply and directly told me he needed me and I came. I always come when Caleb needs me and he's never failed to race to me if I need him.

His brow furrows slightly as he stares at my lips. His own tongue darts out and for the briefest of moments I wonder if he's about to lean down to swipe his full lips over mine. He shakes his head slightly before he tips his head back to look at the grey painted ceiling of the stairwell.

"Just tell me," I whisper. "What is it? Did you do something?"

"I was pushed into a corner," he pauses as his hand drops to his side. "He didn't leave me a choice."

My eyes fall to the floor. I brace myself for what I know is coming next. I don't know why I didn't see the freight train that is Caleb's completely dysfunctional family barreling down the track right towards me. The brothers haven't gotten into an argument in weeks. That's what this is about. It has to be. "It's Asher, isn't it? Is he alright?"

"He's fine," he says through a heavy sigh. "Give me a minute to explain and I'll…"

My stomach twists into a tight knot as I brush past him to reach for the handrail. "What happened? What did you do to him? Is he at the office?"

"Don't go." He gestures towards the concrete stairs. "We need to talk about this. I need you to understand what he did."

"You know how hard it's been for him." I spit out the words. "What if he starts using again? He's been clean for almost six months."

"I'm not responsible for his choices." He tugs at my elbow. "It's his own fault that he was arrested."

"He was arrested?" I turn so quickly on my heel that I have to reach for his arm to find my balance. "When was he arrested?"

"It was right before noon at the corporate office." His jaw tightens. "We didn't have a choice. He was out of control."

"No." I push against his hands but his grasp doesn't lessen at all. "You didn't do that to him. Tell me you didn't have your brother arrested."

"Technically I wasn't the one who made the call to the police," he points out. "My assistant did it."

"Don't do that." I stomp my foot against the concrete floor in exasperation. "Don't divert. Why would you do something like that? We're supposed to be helping him."

"I have gone out of my way to help him." His hand flexes as he grips the handrail. "I've done more for him than anyone else ever has."

The words bite through me. Caleb knows that I carry a burden of guilt with me. I wasn't there for Asher when he needed me in college. I'd turned my back on him at a time when he felt desperately alone. I've never forgiven myself for it.

"You had him arrested, Caleb." I push my finger into his hard chest. "How the hell is that helping him?"

"He was lashing out." He grabs my hand and holds it tightly in his. "I had to step in before he hurt himself or someone else."

"This is unbelievable." I feel my pulse race as I yank my hand free. "I can't believe you'd do this."

"Believe it." He turns towards the door of the stairwell. "He's in jail and this time he's going to have to figure it out on his own."

TWO

"Does Gabriel know?" I follow Caleb's large frame back into his apartment. "Gabriel will know what to do."

"Gabriel is in Italy." His hands run over the lapels of his dark grey suit jacket as he turns to look at me. "He doesn't need to know about this. It's been handled. That's final."

I lower myself into one of the chairs in Caleb's living room. The apartment he lives in is extravagant, yet tastefully decorated. Caleb flaunts his wealth. He's never been ashamed of the fact that his parents built a clothing empire from the ground up. They had handed the keys to their fashion kingdom to their three sons when they divorced. Gabriel, Caleb's older brother, had taken over much of the day-to-day duties. His head is always in the game, which explains why he's in Italy. Right now, it is fashion week in Milan and one of the designers they brought on board last year is making big waves.

Asher, Caleb's younger brother, couldn't shoulder the responsibility that came with being thrown into the position of Director of Sales before he even graduated from college. He was still reeling from his parents' divorce when he was forced to take on a corporate role he wasn't ready for. The luxuries and attention that came with the position were too much and he'd fallen into a life that was filled with reckless abandon. He was rarely lucid and would spend days locked in his apartment with women he'd pick up in clubs and the drugs they brought with them. Gabriel had been able to convince Asher to check himself into a rehab facility nine months ago. He'd come back refreshed, strong and determined to make both of his parents proud. Although Caleb and he didn't always agree on business dealings, they both have the same focus, which is building and expanding the brand their parents began.

"We have to tell Gabriel," I point out as I begin to tap out a text message to Gabriel Foster on my smartphone. "He'd want to know. He's so close to Asher."

I don't look up as I feel him approach me. I know the words have to sting him. Caleb's sole focus for much of his adult life has been the business. He'd watched his twenty-three-year old brother come apart at the seams and the only thing he seemed concerned about at the time was keeping it all away from the sharp eye of the media and the judgmental glances of the public. Keeping the Foster brand untarnished had been his main goal and it had splintered his relationship with his family whether he wants to admit it or not.

"Don't text Gabriel." He gestures towards my phone. "I need him in Milan. If he comes back here, he'll fuck up everything."

I look up into his face. I want to tell him that he's the one who fucked up everything. Having Asher arrested crosses a line that Gabriel won't tolerate. I know that. I've been witness to the shifting dynamics between the three brothers for years. I went to college with Asher and even though he was a year behind me, we spent hours together talking about his family and the unique, and often, volatile connections they all had. It made me feel better about the relationship I share with my own brother, Miles. I thought we had issues when we missed one another's birthdays or failed to connect around the holidays, but being friends with the Fosters has shown me that I have nothing to complain about. I know without question, that Miles would never have me arrested.

"Have you told your parents?" It's a question that I already know the answer to. Caleb and Asher never see eye-to-eye anymore and until a few years ago their parents were the go-to referees. Once they started threatening that they'd hire people from outside the family to run the organization, the brothers hid their battles behind closed doors for the most part. Or they had, until today, when the police were called in.

He scratches his index finger behind his ear. "I'm not telling them. Asher won't either. He knows that his job is gone if they find out he's in trouble."

"What happened?" I rest my smartphone on my lap. "Tell me what happened."

He moves to the left before lowering himself onto the edge of the stainless steel coffee table. He's sitting directly in front of me now. His knees brushing against my calf as he fidgets in place. "He was off when he came into the office this morning. He was late. He's never late."

"How late?" I ask not because it matters in the slightest. It's just habit for me. My logical mind needs to have every piece of available information in front of me in order for me to absorb it.

"He's always in before me." He slides his suit jacket off before tossing it onto the table. "I got in at nine and he wasn't there."

After he completed his therapy, Asher had jumped into his position working alongside his brothers with a ferocity that shocked everyone, including Caleb. He worked late, and on weekends, to keep the sales force motivated. He didn't trust himself to travel to the boutiques that were located outside Manhattan. He hired regional managers for that. I was impressed with his dedication. I was amazed by his desire to overcome his past so he could prove to his family that he was worthy of the trust they had placed in his potential.

"Rowan." Caleb taps my knee. "Just before noon I could hear him berating one of his assistants. Everyone in the office could hear it."

Asher isn't an aggressive person. I've seen him disappointed and even despondent at times and instead of acting on that, he'll retreat into himself. I've never been witness to who he transforms into when he's using heroine. I've never wanted to see that. It would steal away my memories of the boy who would push me on the swings when we were children or the guy who set me up with his best friend in high school.

I know the dark parts of him creep to the surface when he's pumping himself full of drugs. If he was berating his assistant, he wasn't himself. Asher is kind and soft spoken. His soul is quiet and giving.

"You had him arrested because he was yelling at someone?" I push my back into the chair. "You should have sent him home to cool off."

Caleb rubs his hand over his brow. "If that was all it was, I would have taken him home myself until he calmed down."

"There's more?" I ask, not wanting to sound as desperately eager for details as I am. "What else happened?"

"He was pushing things off of his desk," he says the words calmly. "His assistant was cowering in the corner. She was crying, Rowan. She was terrified of him."

It's futile for me to try and conjure up a mental picture of Asher in the middle of a fit of rage. "That doesn't sound like him."

He rests his hand on the edge of the chair I'm sitting in. "I've never seen him that way. I tried to calm him down but he wouldn't stop."

"So you called the police?" It sounds more accusatory than I intend. Caleb can't handle confrontation, which is one of the reasons why he flakes out on relationships. In the past I've heard the tortured and emotional ramblings of women he's dated after Caleb's gone silent on them. Instead of calling them to meet to end the relationship with grace and respect, he ignored them until they finally gave up on him. Considering the fact that more than a few of those women were also my friends, it pulled at the foundation of my friendship with Caleb. I'd railed on him about it enough that when he decided to end things with his last girlfriend, he found a shred of compassion and called her to wish her well before he told her he never wanted to see her again.

"He lunged at someone, Rowan." His voice is steady as he pushes the words out in a low tone. "He attacked one of the junior buyers who ran into the room. I had to step in." Were they hurt?" I cover my eyes with my hands. "Please tell me he didn't hurt anyone."

I feel his large hand race over my knee. "He wasn't hurt. Asher pushed him onto the floor. I stepped in and wrestled him to the ground."

"That's when the police were called?"

"I needed help to control him." I sense the resignation in his tone. "We had to call them. I didn't want him to hurt anyone else or himself. It was obvious he had taken something or shot himself up before he came in. Christ, I had no choice. I did what needed to be done."

THREE

"Where is he now?" I move forward hoping that Caleb takes the hint and retreats so I have the room I need to stand. "I should go see him."

"He'll be arraigned later today or tomorrow." He shifts back moving his body slightly. "You shouldn't go see him."

Caleb has never fully understood my friendship with his brother. When we were children our parents were next door neighbors. I can't remember a time when Gabriel, Caleb and Asher weren't a part of my life. My connection to each of the brothers is different but the common thread is the bond that we forged when we were kids. We each went our own way as we journeyed into our teenage years, but my friendship with Asher has never wavered. Some might say he's like a brother to me but it's never felt that way to either of us. He's one of the people I value most on this earth. I'm protective of him. I feel that even more now knowing he's likely sitting at a police station somewhere in the city.

"Arraigned? Someone is pressing charges?" I pull myself to my feet before I skim my hands over my skirt, trying to smooth out the wrinkled fabric. "Did you get him a lawyer?"

"No." He's on his feet now too. "He'll figure it out."

I look up into his face. I want to see a brief flash of compassion or concern, but those things aren't a part of the landscape of his features. He's stoic and calm. It's unnerving to know that when I walked into this apartment earlier that he was talking to a woman casually about sex, or perhaps it's more appropriate to label it as what it is, casual sex. That shouldn't surprise me. I know the number of intimate partners I've had is only a fraction of the number of women Caleb's been with. He's never propositioned me and at moments like this, I'm glad. I don't doubt that he'd be incredible in bed but what he may make up for there, he's definitely lacking within his heart.

"He'll figure it out on his own?" I rub my hand against his arm wanting him to clear a path so I can finally leave. "You can't be serious."

"I can't keep fixing his mistakes," he spits back at me. "I thought you of all people would understand that."

The words pull me back to the stairwell when he told me that I'd be the only person who would understand what he'd done. He's delusional if he thinks I'm going to pat him on the back for having his brother arrested. I doubt that he recognizes the consequences of what he's done and the lasting impact it will have on Asher's life.

"Why would I understand?" I turn towards him, tapping the toe of my shoe against the floor. "How the hell am I supposed to understand any of this?"

"You're the one who told Asher that life only gives him so many chances." His finger darts into the narrow space between us. "He doesn't get another chance this time, Rowan."

I push my hair back over my shoulder. "I didn't mean having him thrown in jail, Caleb. You know that's not what I meant."

"You meant exactly that." His finger wavers precariously close to my nose. "Rehab obviously didn't work. Talking to him does nothing. Maybe getting arrested will give him the dose of reality he needs."

"Or maybe," I begin before I push my way past him. "Just maybe this will send him back into a tailspin."

"He was already in a tailspin." He reaches for my shoulder. "He'll work out a deal that will require that he goes back to rehab. This is actually a good thing, Rowan."

"It's not a good thing." I turn on my heel to walk away. "You know how scared I am that he'll overdose. You know why that terrifies me and yet you have him arrested."

He throws his head back with a heavy sigh. "He's not going to overdose. You're not seeing this clearly. I thought you wanted what was best for him."

I doubt that anything I say will push Caleb off the righteous throne he's built for himself in his mind. "I need to go. I have to take care of things."

"What things?" He steps in front of me, blocking my path. "Don't go down there and fix this for him."

Wincing at his words, I look up into his face. "He needs someone right now and Gabriel isn't here. If you're not going to help him, I will."

"Don't call Gabriel into this." He rakes his hand through his short, dark hair. "He needs to be focused in Milan right now. We'll lose valuable contacts if he rushes back here."

His attention is on the strength of the business and there's absolutely no reason for me to be surprised by that. I cast my gaze down to the floor. "I won't tell Gabriel until he's back."

"Go do what you want then," he says huskily as he swings his arm towards the apartment door. "I can't stop you from running to save him."

His words bite. They're the same words he threw at me when the man I lived with right after I graduated from college let me down. Caleb warned me that the relationship would end with my heart broken. He was right then. The difference now is that I know that Asher wants to fight his way through his addictions. He just needs someone to stand by his side and if Caleb won't do it, I will.

FOUR

"Where have you been?" Clive Parker, my boss, greets me the moment I step off of the elevator on the thirty-seventh floor of the Corteck building. I've worked side-by-side with Clive for the past three years since I graduated with a degree in business. I may have gotten the job initially because of Clive's friendship with my brother, but since then, I've proven over and over again that I am a valuable asset. I've steadily climbed up the ranks in the company and now I proudly wear the distinction of being one of the few twenty-five-year-old Chief Administrators working in the tech field.

"Hey," I say as I step out of the lift. Anyone else working at Corteck may absorb Clive's tone as brusque, but I know him better than that. "I had to go see a friend."

His eyes briefly scan my face before he pushes a file folder into my hands. "I need you to take a look at this before the end of the day."

I know what it is. It's the proposal that Clive had drawn up to purchase an up and coming tech development company that is based in Chicago. The man has an innate ability to recognize potential. I stick as close to him as I can because I want to soak up every bit of knowledge that he tosses in my direction. Instinctively I know that when he's made a decision, there's little I can do to change his mind, but I still feel a silent victory each time he asks for my opinion. "I'll look at it as soon as I'm in my office."

"Rowan," he says my name quietly, forcing me to turn to face him. "What friend did you go to see?"

Clive's interest in my personal life began the day I started working for him. I know that it's based on my older brother's concern for my well being. Miles was here at Corteck on my very first day, telling Clive that he expected him to take care of me. It was touching and misplaced considering the fact that for the past few years, I've been the one lending an ear, and a shoulder, to Miles.

"Was it Caleb Foster?" he pushes before I have a chance to weave an excuse that would pull his attention away from where I was earlier.

"Yes," I admit. "He needed to talk to me about something."

He rubs the fingers of his left hand over his right palm. "You're upset. I saw it when the elevator doors opened. What did he say to you?"

Clive knows about my mottled history with Caleb. He also knows that I stand by my friends, through thick and thin although right now I'm questioning whether my relationship with Caleb will survive this. "It doesn't matter. I should never have gone to see him in the middle of the day."

A small smirk tugs at the corner of his lips. "Caleb is notorious for calling you to his office for no good reason. Is that what happened today?"

I wish that was what had happened. I wish I could rewind my day to the moment when Caleb called me. I would have told him that I was too busy. Hearing him tell me that Asher was arrested has derailed me completely. I may look mildly frustrated to Clive but the truth is that I'm completely unhinged inside. I actually considered taking the subway to my apartment instead of coming back to work. I scrub my hand over the back of my neck, hoping that I'll find something to say that won't give away the fact that right now I can't even form the sounds to say Caleb's name audibly because I'm so completely pissed off at him.

"Look, Rowan, I get that it's not my business," he begins before he nods down the long corridor towards his private offices. "I know that Caleb can get under your skin. If you need to vent, you know where to find me."

I heave a sigh of relief as I manage a weak grin. "I need to work. Work helps me forget everything."

"Life isn't just about work." He taps me on the hand. "I used to think it was too until I met Lilly."

Lilly is Clive's wife. She's a fiery force to be reckoned with and when she briefly worked at Corteck I saw the barrier that Clive Parker had placed around him melt on the spot. He loves that woman with a fierce determination that I've never seen before. I'd never label myself jealous of the happiness that others have found but it's something I crave. I want a man to feel as desperately drawn to me as Clive does to Lilly.

"Rowan." Thankfully, the head of our security team, Jordan, rounds the corner and calls out my name. "I need to see you."

"There's life outside of these walls." Clive points to the tan painted walls that line the corridor. "Don't work late tonight or any night."

I laugh at the amusement in his tone. He knows that I rarely make it out of the building before seven or eight. "I'll leave when I'm done for the day."

"You'll leave at six today," he counters. "I know you have dinner plans tonight."

"Who told you that?" I purse my lips together and narrow my eyes. "Have you been spying on me?"

"Hardly." He can't contain a deep chuckle. "Ivy was in earlier dropping off Lilly's birthday gift. She told me you two have plans."

"My best friend has a big mouth." I roll my eyes before I settle my gaze on Jordan. "I need to get back to work. I'll stop by your office after I look over the proposal."

"Think about what I said, Rowan." He glances at Jordan as she walks towards us. "Don't bury yourself in your work. One day you'll regret it."

* * *

"I'm not keen on going to Dallas." I tap the pen in my hand against the edge of my desk. "I love Dallas but I have a heavy workload here. Do you think you can handle the trip alone?"

The bright smile that instantly takes over her beautiful face is all the answer I need. Jordan Ayala is the head of cyber security of Corteck. She's the go-to genius I frequently seek out whenever I have a question about any of the new developments our security team is working on. She's brilliant and when she's not dazzling everyone at the office with her mind, she's at home with her husband and five-year-old son.

"I'd love to spend part of the weekend there. Is there any possible way we can make it into a retreat for Ricky and me?"

I know the Clive Parker answer to that question would be that she should make the three day trip without her husband so she can focus on work. He'd want her to back in the office on Friday morning but I'm not Clive Parker. "I'll arrange for Ricky to travel with you. You'll leave on Tuesday morning and come back Sunday. Will your mom take care of Dalton?"

"She'd love it, Rowan." She's on her feet, unable to contain her excitement. "Ricky and I haven't had any time alone since he got back."

Her husband, Ricky, was stationed overseas with the military for eighteen months. I'd watched the spirit in her seep out through the worried grimace that was almost always on her face. He's been back for several months now but their relationship has shifted. She's confided in me that they've had to rediscover one another and with a busy pre-schooler underfoot and another baby on the way, their time alone together is typically reserved for the bedroom or infrequent dinners out when they can afford it.

"You go and have a good time." I motion towards the papers strewn over my desk. "All I need you to do is take those two meetings we talked about and we're good."

"You're the best, Rowan." She leans down to wrap her arms around my neck. "You're an amazing friend. You never let me down."

I cling to her as she hugs me. I may be an amazing friend to her but she's not the friend I'm thinking about. I can't stop thinking about

Caleb and Asher. I need to call my attorney before I do anything else. If I have to go down to the courthouse to personally bail Asher out, I'll do it. He needs me and if I let him down now, I may regret that decision for the rest of my life.

FIVE

"I don't understand what you mean," I try not to sound as utterly confused as I am. "That makes absolutely no sense. His brother told me that he was arrested this morning."

"The charges were dropped." She peers over the top of her reading glasses at me. "Technically he was never actually charged."

I'd called my family's go-to attorney, Devon Princeton, as soon as Jordan left my office. I'd explained the details of Asher's situation to her. Devon isn't a criminal defense attorney. The most notorious case she ever worked on was handling the preparation of my grandparents' wills and helping them decide if Miles or I was entitled to the crystal vase some distant relative gave them at their wedding more than fifty-five years ago. She told me she'd call me back within a couple of hours, but I couldn't wait. I'd taken the subway uptown to her office hoping that

I could garner the name of a criminal defense attorney from her so I could get Asher out of jail before the end of the day.

"The person who filed the charges, dropped them?" I'm not a lawyer but I do have a firm grasp on the basics. I can't claim that all of that is knowledge that I've gained through my time at Corteck. I have sat in a few meetings with our head legal counsel, Imogen Ford, when she was explaining corporate legal documents to me. She wouldn't have had a clue about what I could do to help Asher. I knew Devon would have some insight considering the fact that her son was arrested for marijuana possession outside of his high school just last fall.

"That's what my contact at the police station told me." Her eyebrows dance around playfully, which is enough of a warning for me. I refuse to ask her about her contact. I can only imagine the details she'd gleefully supply to me.

"When was he released?" I glance down at my smartphone. It's almost six now which means that I have two hours before I need to be at Ivy's apartment.

"That I'm not sure about." She nods towards her desk phone. "If you give me three minutes and some privacy I can find out."

I sigh audibly as I turn on my heel to walk out of her office. I close the door behind me before I plop myself down on one of the uncomfortable plastic chairs in the waiting room.

* * *

"You didn't see him today at all?" I tap my hand on the small reception desk in the lobby of Asher's building. "He should have come home within the last two hours. Can you try and buzz him again?"

"You bet, Ms. Bell," Frank, the doorman who keeps a watchful eye over Asher, nods as he swipes his fingers along the screen of the tablet in his hand. "I've been here since three. I haven't left my post at all. Mr. Foster didn't come home."

Asher was released from custody more than two hours ago. He had been held at a police station near Wall Street. I'd raced down there when Devon told me the address. My hope, although short-lived, was that Asher would have been distraught and would have sat himself in one of the chairs in the lobby there. When I burst through the doors and scanned the faces, his was nowhere to be found. I'd tried to call him and it had immediately gone to voicemail. I'd tried twice more since then with exactly the same results.

"He's still not answering the buzzer. If you want, I'll let you up and you can knock on his door."

Before I can form a coherent response I'm walking towards the bank of elevators with Frank hot on my heel. I tip my chin in his direction as he follows me into one of the cars before he pushes a small silver key into the control panel. "This will take you up to the sixth floor. You know his apartment number, right?"

"I know it." I manage a weak grin as he steps back before the doors slam shut.

* * *

"Where's Caleb?" I pull in a deep breath as I step through the doorway. There is absolutely no mistaking the panic in my tone. I'd knocked on Asher's door for more than fifteen minutes before finally giving up. As I rode the elevator back down to the lobby of his building I realized that I only had one more place to go. I had to come back to Caleb's apartment so I hailed a taxi and headed straight over.

I don't consider myself influential but I'm hopeful that what I said to Caleb earlier resonated enough that he made the decision to help Asher. I want the younger Foster brother to be here, resting in bed or watching television. I want him to be safe.

"Who are you? Who let you up here?"

I turn to face the woman asking the questions. She's significantly older than me, which probably means she's not here in a capacity other than professional. I know Caleb's type and this woman isn't it.

"I'm Rowan Bell. I'm a friend of Caleb's." I stop to think about that last statement. "The doorman knows me. He let me up."

"You're a friend of Caleb's?" she parrots the words back to me. "I've never heard of you."

I should take some degree of offense at that but I can't. In a social sense, Caleb and I cross paths only several times a year at various benefit dinners or events. We don't share many of the same friends and while he's out trolling bars and clubs for his next bedmate, I'm generally home by ten going over work that I didn't have time for in the office. We don't travel in the same circles. Our friendship is typically focused on text messages, phone calls and the occasional lunch or drink after work.

"Are you one of his girls?" She eyes me closely. "A lot of you show up here."

Isn't that nice? This random stranger who is standing guard at Caleb's doorway thinks that I'm here because I can't resist him. "I'm not one of his girls."

"Do you think you're special to him?" She leans in so close that I can spot a few wayward dark hairs darting out of her nostrils. "You all think you're so special to him."

If resentment had a spokeswoman, I'd nominate this person for the job. What the hell is her problem? If I had to guess it's that she propositioned Caleb and he unceremoniously turned her down.

"Who are you?" I have just as might right to interrogate her, as she has to question me. "Caleb has never mentioned you before either."

She takes a step back before her tongue juts out to run over her bottom lip. "I'm Ruby. I'm the new house manager."

"Caleb has a house manager? Since when?" The bigger question is why. Caleb lives in this spacious apartment all alone. He may have a guest stay over from time-to-time, or more likely every night, but there's no reason for him to have someone to manage that. He's wasteful. It's just another reason why we're so utterly mismatched.

"I started last month." She glances down at the gold wristwatch on her arm.

"Where were you earlier?" I nod towards her. "I didn't see you here this afternoon."

"I was running errands for Caleb," she says it with so much pride it's as if she ventured out on a journey to bring back lifesaving supplies.

I shake my head slightly. "Where is he? I need to talk to him."

"He's not here." She shifts to the right on her feet before pulling her index finger over the dusty surface of a small table that is placed in the foyer. "I need to address this."

I need to find Caleb, or more importantly, I need to find Asher. "Do you know where he is"He's on a date." The words leave her lips just as I feel my smartphone vibrate in my hand.

I look down and I finally feel my lungs fill with air. It's Asher. He's calling and I may just get all the answers I need.

SIX

"Why aren't we at Axel NY?" Ivy Marlow says as she glances around the vibrantly colored Italian eatery that is only blocks away from her apartment. "I made the reservation for Axel myself last week, Rowan."

She did. I can't argue that point. Axel is Ivy's favorite restaurant in all of Manhattan. It's actually the first choice of many of the people I know, including Caleb. I have little doubt that he's there right now, sitting way too close to his date, drinking a glass of wine and trying to control his raging hard-on. I shake my head to ward off the thought.

When I spoke to Asher on the phone he told me that he hadn't seen Caleb since the police were called to their office. I could hear the regret in his tone. He's staying with a friend tonight. His voice cracked when he asked me if he could stop by my office in the morning.

I suggested we meet briefly this evening, but I could tell he was exhausted. He promised, without the least bit of prompting on my part, that he'd stay in and sleep. Asher knows the devastation that I suffered through because of a man's addictions in the past.

"Something is wrong." She gestures towards me with the half-full glass of house red wine in her hand. "You've been jumpy since you got to my place."

I could argue that I was jumpy because her son decided to use my lap as a mini trampoline. I'd tried to embrace her three-year-old son, Jackson, when I walked through the door but he had another plan in place. He'd dragged me by the hand to an overstuffed leather chair, instructed me to sit and proceeded to use my head as leverage as he bounced on my lap. Right now my thighs are on fire. I was going to swing by the yoga studio for a class in the morning to try and relax, but I doubt I'll even be able to bend my legs at all. Jackson is the sweetest boy I've ever met, but he's not a lightweight. The boy is built like his father. He's strong and sturdy and judging by the warm embrace he gave me before I left, his heart is just as big as Jax Walker's heart is.

"How's Jax?" I try to change the subject by shifting it to her husband. "Why wasn't he at home?"

She peers over the edge of the wine glass. "He's meeting with a business associate about a new deal. You never ask about Jax. What's going on?"

"Your sitter seemed nice." I decide that for now, I'm going to play the oblivious card. If Ivy gets enough wine into her petite self, I won't have to stall much longer. The girl loves to talk about herself when she's bordering on the edge of intoxication. I should know. That's how I found out about her real hair color, the unwanted details about the time Jax fucked her in the corridor of an office building and how she giggles whenever she has a pedicure. She's adorable when she drinks too much so if it happens tonight, I'm definitely not going to complain. I need a distraction and tipsy Ivy may be exactly the perfect thing.

"We're not going to talk about her." She places the glass down. "You know you can tell me anything. Did something happen at work?"

Ivy and I couldn't be more polar opposite about our respective career choices. She's a jewelry designer. Her creativity helped propel her into the position as one of the most sought after designers on the east coast. She has a small storefront and studio named Whispers of Grace in SoHo. The tenor of the space is elegant and sophisticated. I felt an immediate sense of calmness wash over me the first time I walked through the door in search of a gift for my mother. Clive had directed me to Ivy's shop. I hadn't questioned him. I'd followed his advice and I not only found a delicate ruby necklace that day that my mother adores but I found a best friend in Ivy. We hit it off quickly and since that day, almost six months ago, we've become inseparable.

"It's not work," I say handily before taking a first sip of the wine that the server poured for me more than thirty minutes ago. "It's something else."

"Did you meet someone?" She leans her elbows on the worn wooden table.

I'm tempted to confide in her but the undisputed fact of the matter is that Jax is Clive's first cousin and I'm convinced that Ivy tells Jax everything. In the big picture that shouldn't matter but the reality of the situation is that Jax and Clive go for a drink after work at least once a week. I don't want to have to explain to my boss why I didn't tell him that Caleb had called the police on his brother. Clive wants what is best for me, and he believes that Caleb is bad news. After today, I'd have to agree with him but I'm not ready to admit that to him just yet.

"I haven't met anyone," I confess. "I haven't been on a date in months, Ivy."

"I know someone who I think would be perfect for you." She takes another heavy mouthful of wine. "You'd like him. He has tats."

"Tats?" I try to hold back a laugh. "What are tats?"

"Tattoos," she says with effortless ease.

"You call them tats now?" I tease. "What's up with that?"

"Everyone calls them tats." She raises a brow. "He's got them and he's hot."

I can't stop myself from rolling my head back as I giggle. "Your definition of hot isn't the same as mine."

"I know you think Jax is hot." She tips the now empty wine glass in her hand in my direction. "I saw you checking him out the first time you met him."

Dammit. I thought I'd gotten away with that. I had checked him out before I realized he was happily married. It was impossible not to gawk at the man when you catch your first glimpse of him. He's handsome, he knows he is and he's just edging on cultured. Ivy's lucky. I don't have to tell her that. She's the one who is constantly sending me text messages about the daises Jax brings her every few days. Add that to the fact that he can't stop staring at her whenever they're in a room together and I'd say that she found the last perfect man on earth.

"Tell me about the man with the tats." I motion towards the server. "Who is he?"

"His name is Tyler Monroe."

"Tyler Monroe," I repeat it back as I try and place it within my mind. I don't think I've ever heard Ivy mention him before. "How do you know him?"

"He's working on a restaurant deal with Jax." She points around the quaint, but cluttered, interior of the space we're sitting in. "It's not like this. It's more like Axel. Tyler is part owner. He's the chef too."

A man who can cook who has tattoos? That's the opposite of what I usually look for in a man but since I haven't been on a date, or had sex, in months; I'm going to venture outside my typical type. "Do you think he'd be interested in me?"

"Um...let me see." She leans back in the wooden chair and crosses her arms over her chest. "You're tall. You must be at least five foot eight. You're a gorgeous brunette. You have the prettiest blue eyes I've ever seen and your body is killer."

That's the most compliments I've received in a single breath in...well, ever," I half-tease. "When you tell the chef about me, say those exact things."

"I've already told the chef about you." She pulls her large purse into her lap. "I showed him a picture of you."

"You what?" I should be offended but I'm not. I don't typically do blind dates even when I've seen a picture of the man I'm meeting. I've always meet men organically. I met my last boyfriend at a sandwich shop on the Upper West Side. The guy before that I met at the gym. I've never lacked for the attention of men but since I've gotten more immersed in work, I haven't followed up on any of the obvious flirting glances men have been tossing at me.

"This one." She shoves her smartphone into my hands. "I took that a few weeks ago when you were playing with Jackson at the zoo."

My eyes dart down to the screen. My hair is pulled back into a tight ponytail on the top of my head. I'm not wearing any make-up and the jeans and oversized grey sweater I'm wearing is doing little to accentuate anything. I look like a woman who rolled out of bed, pulled on her mother's clothes and wandered out into the free world. "Ivy, this is horrible. You don't have a better picture of me than this?"

She shakes her head slightly from side-to-side. "There isn't a better picture of you than that. You look amazing."

"I look hideous." I push the phone back at her. "If you're going to set me up with anyone, the least you can do is show a decent picture of me."

"He thinks you're beautiful," she says quietly as she looks down. "He said you were breathtaking, Rowan."

SEVEN

Breathtaking? I'd never describe myself that way. I'm not the type of person to stand exposed in front of a full-length mirror so I can find fault with the parts of me that others may not deem perfect. I've always embraced who I am. I like my body and I've never shied away from sharing it with a man when I feel close to him.

I've been with men who've told me that I'm pretty, cute and even adorable. I dated a guy in college who never failed to mention that he loved blondes, but there was something irresistible about me. I grabbed tightly to those words until I caught him in his dorm room with a blonde.

I don't need a man's approval. That's not what I'm looking for. I am looking for a man who appreciates me exactly the way I am.

"Why are you staring at yourself in the mirror?" My roommate, Graham, pops into view behind my reflection. "You're not going to tell me that you're getting a boob job, are you?"

That's the reason I live with him. Ivy had introduced me to Graham the day after I met her. He used to work for the jewelry company that commissioned Ivy's pieces before she ventured out on her own. After leaving New York to pursue his happily-ever-after dream in Seattle with his husband, Graham had landed back here while in the midst of a nasty divorce. He needed a friend and a place to stay. I needed the other half of the rent when my last roommate left without notice. It was a match made in renter's heaven and within the past few months, Graham and I have become close friends.

"You don't think they're big enough?" I turn to face him, jutting my chest out towards him. "Most guys like them."

His eyes settle on the front of my white tank top. "You're not wearing a bra. Doesn't that usually mean your tits are too small if you can wear a shirt like that without a bra?"

I glance down at the tank and the black yoga shorts I put on after I got home from having dinner with Ivy. "It means my bra was too tight."

"I wouldn't change a thing about you." He waves his hand up and down in front of me. "If I was straight, you'd totally be my type."

"You know that's not true," I counter. "If you were straight, Ivy would be your type."

He twists his lips into a mock scowl. "Ivy is a cute little thing, isn't she?"

I nod. "Are you taking off?"

"I'm heading to a club with some friends." He adjusts the buttons of the front of his light blue shirt. "I need to start getting out there again."

He does. I've listened to Graham share the painful details of how his marriage crumbled. He puts on a brave face but I hear him pacing the floors at night. I know that his mind is constantly in high gear. Giving up on a lost love is never easy and for Graham the journey is especially painful since he gave up everything he had here to forge a new life in another state. Sacrifice is romantic until the only payoff is a broken heart and endless pain.

"Have fun." I reach forward to embrace him. "Be careful."

"I love that you worry about me." He brushes his lips against my cheek. "I worry about you too."

"I'm fine." I pull back to look up and into his eyes. "Everything is good in my world."

"Caleb Foster was here earlier." He leans forward so his forehead rests against mine, his brown hair falling into his blue eyes. "He really wanted to talk to you."

"When?" I pull back to look directly at his face. "What time?"

"I was watching one of my Judge shows," he pauses to flash me a gorgeous smile. "It had to have been around six I guess."

"Did he say what he wanted?" I cross my arms over my chest. "It's weird that he didn't try and call me."

He shrugs his left shoulder slightly. "He said he needed to talk to you and when I told him you weren't home from work yet, he mumbled something and took off."

"That's it?" I tilt my head to the side trying to decipher what the hell Caleb wanted.

"If he didn't try and call you, it's nothing." He motions towards where my phone is sitting atop my bed. "Call him and ask him. It's the sure way to find out what he wanted."

"I don't want to talk to him. Something happened today and I'm pissed. "

He rests both of his hands on my shoulders. "I know you've told me there's nothing going on between you and him but there's too much emotion there on both sides for you two to stay friends forever."

I reach up to grab his forearms. "Caleb and I have been friends my entire life. There's nothing there. There will never be anything between us beyond friends and right now I'm not even sure that exists anymore."

"Mark my words, Rowan," he begins before he leans down so he can lower his voice to a whisper. "The two of you want each other. You may not see it, but you feel it. I see it whenever you say his name. I saw it today when he said your name. It's going to happen."

I shake my head as I laugh softly. "I don't want him. I will never sleep with Caleb Foster."

"You're wrong." He drops his hands to his sides. "I can see the smoke that's there between the two of you. You both just need to give the other a chance."

I raise both brows playfully. "This discussion is over. You're going out. I'm going to bed and Caleb won't be in my dreams. I can guarantee that."

EIGHT

"Ruby asked me if we ever fucked each other."

There are at least three things wrong with that statement. The first is the source. That's Caleb Foster's voice. I'd know it anywhere. It's deep, melodic and has just the hint of a growl to it. The second thing is that my office door is wide open. I'm expecting Asher at any minute. I don't need to turn towards the door to know that at least a few of the people I work with heard Caleb's words. The last thing that's completely and totally wrong is that there's no way in hell that Ruby uses the word 'fuck.' I'd peg her for the 'screw' or 'bang' type.

"Caleb," I say his name in barely more than a whisper. "What are you doing here?"

"Have your legs always been that long?"

I smooth my hand over the messy bun I pulled my hair into before I left for work this morning. I'd overslept. After Graham left, I'd fallen between the sheets and had drifted into a deep sleep. I woke with a start when I heard my phone ringing. It was Ivy reminding me that we have a yoga class together the day after tomorrow. Normally I'd tease her about confirming something so far in advance but today, her early call was what I needed to get my ass in gear. I was late to work for the first time in months and now, I have to deal with Caleb. My day can only get better from here.

"Why are you here?" I turn to face him. He's standing in the doorway of my office, his left hand leaning against the doorjamb. His blue suit jacket is draped over his right arm. He looks relaxed, content and way too pleased.

His eyes slowly rake over the red dress I'd hurriedly put on before coming to work. It's shorter than what I'd normally wear but when you're in a rush, you grab the first thing that your hand connects with in the closet. In this case, it's a dress I've worn out on dates a few times. "Is that dress new?"

Any mild discomfort I might have felt when I heard Caleb talk about my legs has been replaced with all out agitation. "No. It's not new."

"You did your hair differently today." He scratches the edge of his jaw. "Why do you look so different?"

This is completely reminiscent of a conversation that we had when I was an adolescent and Caleb saw me in a dress for the first time at the wedding of a mutual friend of our parents. He'd marched over to ask me why I looked so different and I had teased him about it then. Today, I can't push myself into a place where I want there to be anything humorous floating between us. I'm still angry with him over what happened to Asher yesterday.

"I don't look different." I tug on the back of my office chair. "I asked you why you're here."

"Do you have a lunch date?" He finally walks into the room. "You're going out with someone at lunch, aren't you? Do I know him?"

I'm not shocked by the barrage of questions. Caleb has met every man I've ever been in a relationship with. I hadn't planned it that way but circumstances brought him straight into the path of me and my boyfriends in the past. For the most part he's been remarkably cordial to them.

I, on the other hand, have only met one of Caleb's past girlfriends. It was actually his fiancé. Her name is Vena and she's the one woman who found her way into Caleb's heart. Soon after Caleb proposed to her, the relationship was over. We've never talked about it and I doubt we ever will. I only tried once to bring it up and he'd shut me down in anger, telling me to never mention her name again. I hadn't. I won't.

"It's not like I'm going to follow you on your lunch date."

"What?" I pull myself back into the moment. "Did you just say you're going to follow me on my lunch date?"

He puffs out a breath between pursed lips as he takes a seat in one of the chairs opposite my desk. "I said I wouldn't do that. I was just curious about who you're having lunch with."

"I'm not having lunch with anyone." I dart my eyes behind him towards the door. Asher should have been here by now. I'm worried that he caught sight of Caleb in the lobby of the building and decided to ditch me. I need to talk to him. I want to make sure he's alright after what happened yesterday.

Caleb careens his neck to the side. "Who are you looking for? Are you fucking someone who works here? Introduce me to him. I want to meet him."

My hands jump to cover my face. This isn't happening. I can't talk about my non-existent sex life this early in the morning. I certainly can't talk about it with him. "Stop, Caleb. My life isn't your business."

"I didn't think you were dating." He leans forward in the chair. "When did you start dating someone?"

"When did you hire a house manager?" I need to shift the focus of this completely inappropriate conversation. "Why did you hire her?"

"I brought her on board a few weeks ago." He crosses his long legs. "She's a close friend of my mother. She needed a job."

I recognize the irony in the situation. Caleb's loyalties lie in one place. It's not with me or his brothers. It may have been his former fiancé at one point, but it's always been his parents. If they need anything, Caleb is the first to jump to the ready to help. I admired it when we were younger but now I see it clearly for what it is. He's trying to make up for what he views as his part in the breakdown of their marriage. He quietly blamed himself when they announced they were separating. His guilt stemming from the fact that he forced himself into the middle of their business relationship.

"Have you talked to Asher?" I scan my smartphone's screen hoping to see a text from Asher telling me he's running late.

"You only get one phone call in prison," he says with the hint of amusement in his tone. "I doubt I'm Asher's call."

I have to bite my bottom lip to stave off the urge I feel to scream at him. It may be his incessant need to joke about serious situations because he can't handle anything heavy, but this pushes all of my buttons. "Asher isn't in prison."

He taps his foot against the front of my desk. "Did you pay his bail?"

I look into his face. He doesn't deserve an answer. He doesn't deserve another ounce of my time. He went out on a date when he thought his brother was sitting in jail. He carried on with his life, without a single missed step at all. "What happened to you, Caleb?"

"What's that supposed to mean?" He cocks a dark brow as his tongue slides over his bottom lip.

"You've changed so much." I exhale audibly. "I don't know when it happened but you're not the man you used to beThe words hit him with the force of a hurricane. His expression doesn't give anything away but his body language does. His shoulder fall back, his neck surges forward and his gaze drops into his lap. "I haven't changed at all."

"You're selfish," I say it because it's what I see and feel. "The Caleb I used to know would have done everything in his power to protect his brother."

He's on his feet in one quick movement. "I was protecting him, Rowan. I was doing what I needed to do to protect him."

"No," I push the word out slowly and loudly. "You were protecting your precious company's reputation."

"He was in full attack mode." He clenches his fists together at his sides. "You weren't there. You don't know what was going on."

My finger darts out to wave in the air over my desk. "I know that you're at least six inches taller than him. You must have at least fifty pounds on him. You're telling me that you couldn't control him?"

"You don't need to fight my battles, Bell," Asher's voice breaks into our conversation. "Caleb did what he needed to do. I don't blame him. I don't want you to either."

NINE

"Asher," I say his name as I round my desk to embrace him. "I tried to find you yesterday. I've been so worried about you."

"I know." His hands leap to my shoulders. "Frank told me you were at my building. I needed to crash at a friend's house."

"Are you alright?" I step back to soak in the sight of him. There's never been any question Asher, Caleb and Gabriel are brothers. They all have the same dark brown hair and brown eyes. Asher is just as striking to look at as his brothers but he doesn't carry the same confident air that they do. He's shy. He's more reserved and unless you know him well, making eye contact isn't going to happen.

"I'm okay." His gaze moves to the right to where his brother is watching us.

Caleb stands in silence with his broad arms crossed over his chest. I can't tell if he's seething or if he's relieved to see his younger brother looking freshly showered, shaved and ready to take on his day.

"I need to talk to you about something." Asher sighs and pushes his hand through his hair. "I want to talk about it alone."

"I'm leaving," Caleb spits the words out without looking at either of us.

"Caleb," I start before I realize I don't know what to say.

"Don't." His hand juts into the air. "I need to get to work."

I glance quickly at Asher as Caleb walks through the door of my office before he turns to the right and disappears down the corridor.

I reach for Asher's hands and squeeze them both tightly. "Were you hurt? Did you get hurt yesterday?"

"No." He shakes his head rapidly from side-to-side before looking up towards the ceiling. "I lost it. I totally lost it."

I want to ask the obvious question about what he was on but focusing on the elephant that's in the room isn't going to pull any of the details I want out of Asher. I have to pace myself. I can't push him into a corner. If I do that, he'll never view me as someone he can confide in. "I wanted to call Gabriel. I really wanted to call him to help."

His eyes search mine briefly. "He's in Italy. He's got too much to worry about already."

I nod. "Caleb told me that."

His jaw tightens at the mention of his brother's name. "Caleb panicked yesterday. He came at me full force. I lashed out. I think I hurt him."

I smile softly at the idea that Asher could cause any physical damage to his brother. I don't doubt that Asher can defend himself, but I've witnessed Caleb pushing men up against walls with just one hand. "He's fine. You didn't hurt him."

"He called the police." He motions towards the two chairs that are sitting in front of my desk. "Can we sit?"

"Yes." I point towards the door. "I'll close my door. You sit."

I glance down the corridor in the direction Caleb took before I softly close my office door. I can tell that my words stung him. Years ago, I would have raced after him to explain things. Today, although a part of me wants to do that, I can't. Asher needs me and Caleb needs to have some time to absorb what I said.

"You're sure that you're okay?" I tap Asher on the shoulder before I take a seat in the chair next to him. "Do you want anything? I can get you some coffee or a bottle of water?"

"I'm good, Bell," he says my nickname with the same ease he always has. Asher and my father are the only two people who call me that. Caleb did at one point, but as we grew older, and he took on a more serious stance, he dropped it.

"I spoke to my lawyer yesterday," I pause to study his face. "I thought you may need a lawyer, so I went to see mine. She's not a criminal lawyer but she was able to find out that you weren't charged with anything."

His gaze meets mine for a brief second. "You've always been one of my best friends. You know that, right?"

I feel a sudden lump in my throat. "You're one of my best friends too."

"I remember when Tom overdosed." He exhales audibly. "I still remember everything about that day."

Until a few months ago, the mention of my former boyfriend's name would bring a flash of tears to my eyes. I loved Tom. He was brilliant, fun and caught within a world of deep depression. We had met in class during my senior year in college. He had a mess of blonde curls on his head and eyes that were a pale blue. He was introspective, romantic and wore eyeglasses that would always slip off the bridge of his nose.

"I do too." I rub at my chest trying to ease the growing tightness I feel.

"I think about that day whenever I feel the urge." He leans back in the chair. "I've been thinking about that day a lot lately."

Asher had been with me the day I found Tom passed out on the floor of the apartment we were sharing. We'd moved in together after I graduated and as Tom continued his studies towards his Master's in business, he found an ally in cocaine. Asher had warned me twice that he thought Tom was using, but it was easier to ignore the signs and bathe in the good moments. My relationship with Tom was filled with passion and when the dust had settled and he was released from the hospital, he made a choice. He chose the drugs and he's never looked back.

"I think about it sometimes too," I offer back. "I thought about it yesterday."

"I haven't touched anything since I left rehab." He crosses his legs, pulling at the material of his pant leg. "I wasn't on anything yesterday."

If he said those words to Caleb I know that they would be met with disbelief, but Asher wouldn't mask the truth from me. Not about this. He saw, firsthand, how devastated I was when I found out he had been using last year. My instinct then was to abandon him. I hadn't. I'd gone to visit him when he was in rehab and I cried when he told me that he'd let me down.

"I believe you," I say it with conviction. "Caleb said you were angry. He said you were lashing out."

He leans forward to rest his hands on his knees. "Caleb and I are a lot alike. He can't see it. He won't see it."

"You're not that alike," I say jokingly. "Caleb's changed so much. He's not the same person he used to be."

"None of us are." His fingers brush lightly against my knee. "Do you remember how shy you used to be? You'd hide behind the oak tree in front of your parents' townhouse when we called you over to play baseball. I don't think you said two words to me before you hit your tenth birthday."

I'd cowered behind my parents when I was a child. I was painfully unsure of myself. I had only one friend in school but when I'd come home, I'd often find the Foster boys sitting on their front stoop. Gabriel is seven years older than me and back when I was a child, he was the one who would bring me a package of gum from the store or make promises about how he'd run a huge company one day and I would be his second-in-charge. He would tell me that I was the smartest girl he knew even though I doubted the words.

Caleb, the middle child, was always the most beautiful to me. I was drawn to him instantly and once I understood about fairy tales and promised love, I'd fallen for him in my own innocent way. I'd sit by my bedroom window and watch him as he rode his skateboard down the quiet street. I took a hooded sweatshirt he once left on the railing of the stoop so that I could inhale the heady scent of his skin. I still have it. It's tucked into a box at the back of my closet.

Asher and I are closest in age but were the furthest apart when we were children. He was as shy as me and on the rare occasions when we did speak to each other, it was stunted. Our words would stall and one of us would inevitably drift away from the discussion as soon as the chance was upon us. He reached out when he started college and our friendship found its foundation then. Our life choices didn't mirror one another's and as he wandered into a world filled with temptation and pain, I'd focused on my studies and work. We'd let each other down. We both knew it even if we hadn't actually admitted it to one another.

"I wasn't using anything yesterday, Bell," he says bluntly as he taps his finger on my knee. "I was upset about something."

I draw my gaze up to meet his. I study his face. His skin is sallow, his eyes sunken in. He may have showered, shaved and put on a brave face, but there's something lurking beneath the surface. "What were you upset about?"

"I got some news," he says wearily. "I had to stop by…I went to see someone yesterday morning before work and it…the conversation upset me."

The disjointed answer is punctuated by the pained expression on his face. I want to ask him to just spit it out but Asher has always needed a barrier between him and everyone else. It's how he deals with anything that overwhelms him. He used to turn to drugs, but rehab and ongoing therapy have taught him how to cope.

"We can talk about it if you want."

"I don't want to talk about it right now." He shifts in the chair. "I want to talk about Caleb."

"Caleb?" I ask through a deep, and audible, sigh. "Why would we talk about him?"

"He needs you. My brother needs you, Bell."

TEN

"Caleb only needs one person and that's himself," I say with complete conviction. "He doesn't need me. He doesn't need anyone."

"You're wrong." Asher points at me. "When the police handcuffed me yesterday, Caleb kept talking about calling you to tell you what happened."

"That was his guilty conscience talking," I counter. "He actually told me that I'm the only person who would understand why he had you arrested. How am I supposed to understand it? I honestly don't understand Caleb at all anymore."

"He was scared." He half-shrugs his shoulder. "I've never seen him that scared. He didn't know what to do, Bell. He pinned me on the ground."

"He could have really hurt you," I cringe as I say the words. I was witness to Caleb defending himself at a club in Hell's Kitchen one night almost two years ago. I was there with friends and once I heard that there was a scuffle on the street, I joined the crowd that was scurrying outside to get a glimpse. I was shocked to see Caleb pushing a stranger against the brick wall of the building while he pummeled the man's head with his fist. It's an image I can't shed. Caleb's never divulged the details of what drove him to the edge of losing control, but I know now that it's within him to take a life, whether he admits it or not.

"Caleb would never hurt me," he says grimly. "I think he thought I was on something."

It's not a preposterous conclusion to jump to. Both Caleb and Gabriel have held their breath the past few months hoping that Asher wouldn't fall back into his addiction. He's fought against it, and even though Asher has confided in me that Gabriel is proud of him, Caleb hasn't offered his reassurance that he believes his younger brother is on the right track. I know it pains Asher. He's told me as much.

"It doesn't matter what Caleb thinks." I pull on the hem of my dress, wishing I had taken the extra three minutes I needed to pick out another outfit before I raced to work. "You're not taking anything."

"I'm tempted," he admits quietly. "There's way too much temptation here."

I can't respond in any way other than honestly. My only vice is a glass of wine now and again and the occasional pair of expensive shoes. I've never felt drawn to try any illicit drugs. It's not because I've never been curious. It's simply because I'm too focused on my work and my goals. I don't do distractions.

"In New York, you mean?" I ask.

"This is one of the worst places for someone like me," he chuckles. "I go to meetings every day. I'm there sometimes two or three times a day but the draw is right there. It's always right there."

I nod. I may not understand the physical need to indulge, but I know what it feels like to crave something or someone. I've felt intense longings in my life but they've always been about men that were wrong for me. That's not comparable to what Asher feels, but it's the only experience I have to draw from.

"Can I help?" I ask even though I know that I can't. I've offered time and time again but although Asher and I may be close friends, our worlds beyond that don't collide.

"I think I'm going to take off for a few weeks." He gestures towards the large window in my office. "I've been thinking about going to see my mom."

Giana Foster had fled New York for the sanctity of her childhood home in Brussels after her divorce. Roman, her husband, had found not only opportunity and fortune in his business but a bevy of beautiful, young models willing to do almost anything to land the coveted spot of a place in the print campaign for the family's female fashion brand, Arilia. They'd named their first boutique after Giana's mother and now, twenty-five years later, they'd nurtured that brand along with the men's fashion line, Berdine, into a billion dollar business.

"Really?" I can't contain my surprise. "I think that's a great idea."

"Caleb fired me yesterday," He shakes his head in mock disbelief. "That means I'm going to have a lot of extra time on my hands. A trip to Brussels would be good."

I know he's likely right but I also know that Caleb wasn't serious when he fired him. "Caleb probably didn't mean it. I mean, I doubt that you're actually fired."

"I work there because I'm a Foster." He claps his hands together. "Don't get me wrong. I like the job. I'm good at it, but it's sucking the life out of me."

It's the first time I've heard him audibly express what I've been wondering for months. "You don't like your job?"

"Honestly." He tips his chin towards me. "I do it because my parents want to me to do it. I do it because it's their legacy. I don't even wear our clothes."

I laugh at the admission. "I don't either."

"I like that about you." He chuckles. "Remember when Caleb told you to go into the store on West 57th Street and pick anything you wanted? You never showed up."

I remember that day vividly. It was right before I started at Corteck. I was panicked because my work wardrobe consisted of the navy blue suit I'd worn to countless interviews, two white blouses, a pair of black slacks and a worn red pencil skirt. When I'd told Caleb I landed the job he first lectured me on the merits of working for him before he insisted I visit one of the Arilia stores to choose a new wardrobe as a graduation gift from the Fosters for me. I hadn't. I'd worn the few items I had to the office until I received my first paycheck and then I went to an outlet mall in New Jersey to buy dozens of items that were all discounted heavily. Caleb had been both livid, and mildly impressed, with my determination to get the most out of every dollar I earned.

"He's always tried to take care of you." Asher's lip slide into a smile. "You know he cares about your opinion more than anyone else's."

I've thought that at times. It's mainly been when Caleb's shown up at my office in the middle of the day with a scowl on his face and a desperate need to be reassured that he'd made the right decision about a new location or because he'd changed suppliers and was doubting himself. It's happened with women too. I was the first person he saw after Vena dumped him. He'd arrived at my apartment, completely unexpectedly with beer and pizza and a broken look in his eyes.

"If that were true, he wouldn't have had you arrested," I stop to raise my hand. I know Asher and I know that he's about to argue his brother's side of the story on his behalf. "It went too far. A year or two ago he never would have done that."

"A year or two ago he was in control of everything." He clenches the wooden arms of the chair in his hands. "He's losing control and it's scaring the shit out of him."

ELEVEN

I think I have my act together. I'm never late on my rent or credit card payments. I tuck money into my retirement fund every month and I go see the dentist twice a year to have my teeth cleaned. I don't have a desire to control anything other than my own life. I know it's different for Caleb. It's always been different for him. I've never known him as someone who sits back idly while the world makes choices for him. He takes the bull by the horns and steers it in the direction he wants to go. He's in control of every aspect of not only his own life, but also the lives of the people around him.

"Caleb is a control freak," I spit the words out through a wide smile. "Remember that puppy that Miles and I had when we were kids. Caleb was the one who taught it all those tricks. He's always been in control of everyone and everything."

Asher tugs on the collar of his dress shirt. "He wants to control everyone and everything. He may have been able to do that at one time, but it's not that way anymore. You know that Gabriel hired someone to oversee the European division, right?"

I don't talk business that often with any of the Foster brothers. I pride myself on having a sound business mind, but I have no logical grasp on what it takes to run a clothing conglomerate. Gabriel has always viewed me as the young neighbor girl who followed in his footsteps and went to college to get a business degree. I was actually following in my father's footsteps and when his own plumbing company fell victim to the recession, I had to adjust my focus, which is how I ended up at Corteck.

"I didn't know that," I answer honestly. "Caleb didn't tell me."

"It's pissing Caleb off." He sucks in a quick breath. "He had a trip to London planned. He thinks he can run everything from his office here but he can't. Gabriel went behind his back to set up our team in Europe."

That partially explains Celeb's attitude lately. He's been harsh, frustrated and preoccupied. I assumed it was because of a woman he was seeing. I had no idea that there was that much friction between him and Gabriel.

"He must have been livid." I try not to break a smile. "I'm a little surprised that he didn't call me to complain about it all."

He cocks a dark brow. "I'm surprised too. You're his best friend."

At one point, a year or two ago, I would have taken great comfort in hearing Asher say those words. I've volleyed back and forth between wanting Caleb as a platonic friend to wanting much more with him. I'm not sure if I've ever been in love with him because the only man I know I've loved is Tom and those feelings were so jumbled with resentment over his addiction that they became a hazy mess. I've avoided diving back into anything serious because of that.

"I'm not his best friend," I insist softly. "My best friend wouldn't do some of the shit that he does."

He tilts his head back in laughter. "Caleb's let his success go to his head. I don't dispute that but he's still the same guy you've always known."

"He's not." I hesitate before I continue, "I'm not even sure I want him as a friend anymore. He had you arrested, Asher. You're his brother. You've already been through so much."

"I'm an addict." He leans forward to pull both of my hands into his. "My addictions terrify him. He panicked. He did the only thing he thought would help."

"He was wrong." I look down at my lap. "He knows he was wrong. That's why he made me promise to still be his friend before he told me what happened."

"You're the only constant in my brother's life." His voice is gruff. "You've always been there for him. He needs that. He needs you now more than ever

* * *

"You're not working from home today?" I tap my hand lightly on his shoulder.

"Please be wearing that hot little red dress you had on earlier," he says smugly. "Red is my new favorite color."

I try not to grin as he pivots on his heel to look at me. His eyes settle on the neckline of the dress. It's not low cut but it definitely accentuates the limited cleavage that I do have.

"I didn't have time to go home to change, Caleb."

"I want you to wear that dress every time you come here to see me." He gestures around the empty boardroom we're standing in. "I have a meeting in ten. What's up?"

I stare at his handsome face. There isn't a remnant of the pain that flashed over his expression earlier when he was in my office and I was berating him over how much he's changed. It's always like that with the two of us. We forgive and forget. We always have. "I want to talk about Asher."

His rubs his index finger over his lips. "What about him?"

"You fired him." I sigh heavily. "Why did you fire him?"

He swallows hard before he answers. "He can't work here if he's in jail or in rehab."

"He's not using anything." I glare at him. "He was upset about something. He feels badly about what he did."

This is the point in the conversation when Caleb should admit that he feels badly about what he did too, namely having his brother arrested. That would involve him swallowing his pride and declaring he was wrong too.

Unless hell has frozen over since I walked into this office tower, it's never going to happen.

"You trust him too much, Rowan." His eyes drop to my legs. "You put too much faith in Asher."

"I'm not going to apologize for being his friend." I struggle to not point out that he doesn't put enough faith in his younger brother. "I believe in him."

"You shouldn't." He brushes past me to rest his tablet on the long, rectangular table. "You can't depend on people like him."

I push out a heavy breath at the underlying inference in his words. "What does that mean?"

His gaze is soft as he studies my face. "God, you're beautiful. You're so beautiful and trusting. I don't want you to get hurt. It kills me when you get hurt."

I stare at his lips as he closes them slowly. "Asher isn't going to hurt me. You don't understand our friendship. You don't know what he means to me."

"Tell me then." His hand jumps to my waist. "Tell me exactly what my younger brother means to you."

TWELVE

I work to level my breathing as look into Caleb's eyes. His fingers are sliding softly over the fabric of my dress. I want to explain in pointed detail why he needs to get over what happened yesterday so he can see the potential that Asher has but I can't find those words. "We're friends."

"Yes, Rowan." His breath floats over my cheek as he leans down. "We've established that you and Asher are friends. You and I are friends too but it's different with you and him."

"Different?" I ask before I lick my bottom lip. I feel as though I haven't had anything to drink in days.

"Different," he repeats. "As in not the same."

I nod. "It is different."

I see something flash across his expression but it's too fleeting to place. "How is it different?"

"He's trying," I begin before I smooth my hand over my hair. It's falling from the bun I pushed it into this morning. I didn't take a minute to look at myself in the mirror before I left Corteck. I'd made Asher promise me that he'd let me know before he jetted off to see his mother. Once I said goodbye to him, I'd grabbed my purse and had walked the three blocks to Caleb's office to confront him.

His assistant had pointed me towards the boardroom when I arrived and before I had time to form a plan of action in my head, I was standing behind him, tapping him on the shoulder.

"What's he trying to do?" His lips hover close to mine. "Tell me what he's trying to do."

I close my eyes briefly hoping it will offer me enough of an escape that I can find my composure again. It doesn't work. My heart is racing just as fast once I open them to see Caleb's face. "He's trying to be a good person."

"A good person?" he parrots back. "Asher doesn't know the first thing about being a good person."

I narrow my gaze. "He does. You don't."

He can't control the smile that tugs at the corner of his lips. "You don't think I'm a good person?"

It's a loaded question. I don't doubt that Caleb has the capacity to be kind and giving. I know that he does. Those parts of him have just become buried beneath his drive to prove that he's the best at what he does, both in his professional and personal lives. "You've changed."

"You're wrong. I haven't changed. The people around me have changed."

I don't fall into the radius of the people he's referring to. I know that I don't. I've heard him tell me too often that I'm still the same girl he remembers from when he was a kid. He's talking about his brothers. "You mean Asher and Gabriel?"

"Money changes people." He glances towards the conference table. "Once you give people a taste of it, they can't control their need to have it."

If I didn't know better I'd swear he's talking about himself more than either of his brothers. "I don't have a lot so I don't know."

"You're fortunate." He leans back far enough that I finally feel as though I can breathe. "You can trust your brother. I don't have that luxury anymore."

There's a pain woven into the words that can't be ignored. "They're still your brothers, Caleb. They'll always be your brothers."

"They are my brothers." He nods as his eyes dart to the door I just walked through. "They're also ruthless, Row. You need to watch yourself around them. They'll use you to get to me."

It's a callous remark meant to intimidate me. "Not everything is about you. My friendship with Asher has nothing to do with you."

"It has everything to do with me." He leans so far forward that his lips flutter against the side of my ear. "He told me yesterday when they were handcuffing him that if push comes to shove, you'll choose him over me."

The words resonate the same way they did when we were children and the brothers were picking teams for basketball at the park. We're not doing a schoolyard pick for teams anymore. We're adults and as I watch Caleb raise his arm to summon in a group of his employees into the room I can't help but wonder whether Asher is right. If I had to take sides, I doubt that I'd be standing next to Caleb when the dust finally settled.

THIRTEEN

"Which one have you slept with?" Ivy's hand races over the screen of my laptop. "Was it this one?"

I stare at where she's firmly planted her finger over the image of Gabriel's face on the Foster Enterprises website. "No, that's Gabriel. He's the oldest. I've never even thought about him that way."

"He's totally my type," she whispers as her eyes dart around the crowded diner we're sitting in. "Don't tell my husband I said that."

I laugh out loud. "I won't tell Jax a thing."

"It has to be this one then." She slides her finger over the screen towards Asher's picture. "He's more your type."

"I haven't slept with any of them." I reach to grab the edge of the laptop's screen. I'm not even sure why I brought up the Foster brothers when I agreed to meet Ivy for a coffee after work.

"You're talking technicalities." She gently pushes my hand away. "Do you want to sleep with this one?"

"No." I shake my head from side-to-side. "That's Asher. He's definitely not my type. He's my pal."

"You have a pal that looks like that?" She cocks a perfectly sculpted blonde brow. "None of my pals look like that."

I put my hand over my mouth as I try to stifle a raucous laugh.

"It's the one in the middle then." She nods towards the screen. "Caleb. Caleb Foster."

I pick up the now cool mug of coffee that I'd ordered when we first arrived. I'd listened patiently for twenty minutes while Ivy told me about a custom designed engagement ring she'd been working on all day. I admired the pictures of the piece on her phone and had asked, out of genuine curiosity, about the man who ordered the ring.

As soon as she asked me about my day, I'd launched into a disjointed accounting of my time with both Asher and Caleb. She wanted a visual, so I showed her the brothers' profile images on their website.

"It's that one, right?" she pushes. "He's gorgeous. You've known him how long?"

"I can't remember a time when I didn't know him." I shrug as I place the mug back on the table. "We lived next door to his family when I was growing up."

"So he's like a brother?"

"No," I shake my head fervently. "It's never been like that. We've just been friends."

"Do you want to be more than friends with him?"

My best friend in middle school and a friend in college both asked me the very same question. I've always fallen back on the same answer I'm going to give Ivy now. "I used to have a crush on him but that passed."

The expression on her face makes it clear that she's not buying into a word of what I'm saying. "How old is he?"

"Caleb is thirty."

"Does he want to get married?"

"To me?" I ask without thinking.

She giggles loudly. "Maybe I should be asking if you want to marry him."

"No." I reach for the mug again and this time I take a heavy swallow just to keep my mouth busy.

"Are you attracted to him?" She taps her finger on the checkered tablecloth. "Are you attracted to Caleb?"

Lying would be completely and utterly futile at this point. The mere fact that I got all tongue tied when she asked me whether he wanted to get married is already proof of my confusion regarding him. "He's very attractive, Ivy."

"I'm not going to argue with you about that. Why haven't you just jumped into bed with him?"

It's a question I've asked myself more than once. It definitely hasn't been for lack of opportunity. I know Caleb. I know him well enough to know that there have been moments when he's been open to the idea of sleeping with me. He's never come right out and told me he wants me, but I've seen the same longing I feel for him, reflected back to me. The only problem is that whenever I've gotten up the nerve to think I'll make a move, his interest has waned and my better judgement has kicked in.

"Remember when you first told me about how you met Jax?" I smile across the table at her. "You said he was a ladies' man before that."

"I said he fucked a lot of women before he met me." She tips her chin up. "He never told me how many but it's got to be a pretty high number."

I admire the way she throws out the words without any reservation. She can do that because she's confident in how much Jax loves her now. "Caleb is like that."

"It's normal for men in the city." She gestures around the crowded coffee shop. "They experiment until they find the right one. Once they do, everything changes and they give that up."

It's a sweet sentiment and expected given the way that Ivy views life. She's convinced that every person has a soul mate they're destined to find. I'm more grounded. I think we're bound to make connections in our lives that fill a need. Sometimes those connections last and other times, they fade. I want a relationship like the one Ivy and Jax have, but I'm clear minded enough to know that I may never find that.

"The right one has to be someone you share the same vision with," I say quietly. "Caleb and I are completely different people and I don't want to risk the friendship we do have even though it's hanging by a thread."

"What does that mean?"

"There was a time when I thought Caleb could do no wrong," I admit sheepishly. "I'm not that naïve anymore. I know that no man is perfect but he does things I don't understand, Ivy. It's not just the stuff with his brothers. It's how he uses women and flaunts his wealth. He's not the same boy who used to share an ice cream cone with me when we were kids."

"That boy is still inside of him somewhere." She pats the top of my hand. "The difference now is that he's lost sight of him. You need to help him find that part of him again."

"I don't need to do that." I sigh heavily as I run my finger over the rim of the mug. "He likes who he is. He's happy with the man he is."

"Then you just have to find a way to accept him the way he is."

"Or," I ready myself to say the words. "Maybe I have to walk away from Caleb and our friendship for good."

FOURTEEN

"Why aren't you in Dallas?"

I knew that this conversation was coming. I thought I'd be forced into it yesterday but Clive had taken the day off to spend it with his wife. Typically when he does that, he has a glow about him that lasts for days. Apparently, the glow has already dissipated into the ether.

"I sent Jordan," I say effortlessly without looking up from my laptop screen. "I had too much to do here."

"You sent her husband along for the ride?" He can't mask the obvious amusement in his tone. "Is he on payroll now?"

I know he's asking because it's expected. He's a shrewd and level headed businessman but he does have a heart that most people never get a clear glimpse of. I'm hoping that if I ignore the question he'll move onto another topic of discussion.

"Why did you send Jordan's husband with her?" He traces his index finger over the edge of my laptop. "You know I wouldn't have approved that."

"I know that you trust me to make decisions that benefit the company," I counter. "I saw it as a good investment."

"A good investment?" he asks gruffly. "You're going to need to explain that one to me, Rowan."

I slam my laptop shut before I look up into his face. "Did you cut your hair? It's shorter than normal."

He runs his hand over his hair. "Lilly wanted to see it short. Do you like it?"

"I love it." I nod slightly. "You trimmed your beard too?"

"We had a spa day," he whispers quietly as he leans one hand against my desk. "I swear to God that woman can get me to do anything for her."

"It was a fun day?" I'm not sure why I even ask. The beaming grin on his face is giving everything away.

"One of the best," he answers quickly. "An entire day with the woman I love is a gift to me. I need to do that more. It regenerates me."

"That's why I did it."

"Did what?"

"That's why I sent Jordan and her husband to Dallas together." I push my hands against the side of my desk before I rise to my feet. "She needed to feel that too. She's been dragging her heels around here. Giving her the chance to spend a few days alone with her husband will light a fire underneath her again."

He crosses his arms over his chest as a slight grin tugs at the corner of his mouth. "Well played, Rowan. You're learning."

"She deserves it, Clive." I tip my chin towards him. "She's done a lot of good work this year. I saw it as a bonus. We scratch her back, she'll scratch our back."

"You've convinced me." He throws his hands up in mock defeat. "I should have made you the head of Human Resources."

"No." I round my desk. "I like the job I have."

"What's been going on with you?" He nods towards the open door of my office. "If you need someone to talk to, I've got a few minutes."

He means well even if the offer feels misplaced. "I've got nothing going on. I've just been working and hanging out with Ivy."

"I saw her the other day." He rubs his hand over his brow. "She said she was going to set you up with a business associate of Jax."

"A business associate of her husband?" I repeat back hoping it will jog my memory.

"A chef," he offers. "Tyler something. Ivy said you were anxious to meet him."

Ivy would say that. It has nothing to do with my being anxious to meet him and everything to do with her wanting to see if her sixth sense about matching romantic partners is on par. I'd actually completely forgotten about the potential blind date. "He sounds nice."

"We can do a double date thing if you want. Lilly would love it."

It's a suggestion meant to give me the reassurance I need to jump back into the dating world. Clive knows that I've hidden myself away in my office and in my apartment since my last relationship ended. I'm not the type of woman who seeks out a boyfriend just to have a warm body to cling to at night.

"I'll figure it out. I've never dated a chef before and he is gorgeous." I glance down at my smartphone, which is sitting, atop my desk. "I'll get his number from Ivy and I'll see when he's free to have dinner with me."

"You're having dinner with who?" Caleb's deep voice bounces off of the walls of my office. "If you want someone to have dinner with, I'm available."

* * *

Back in high school if one guy heard me talking about hanging out with another guy, he may have decided that would be the perfect time to swoop in and stake his claim. It's happened to me before. It's never happened with Caleb Foster though. He's actually been excited in the past when I've told him about a new guy I've met. He even arranged for an expensive bottle of champagne to be delivered to my apartment when I had a date with a man last year that I was crazy about. He's never tried to interject himself into my dating life though until this very minute.

"Caleb," Clive turns to face him. "What are you doing here?"

"Clive." Caleb darts his hand into the air. "It's been a long time."

My boss pulls Caleb's hand into a firm shake. "How are things at Foster?"

"They'd be better if Rowan came to work for us," he jokes. "I've been trying to make that happen for years. What's your secret to keeping her here?"

I cough loudly hoping it will be enough of a deterrent to keep Clive from saying anything that will set Caleb off.

"I'll leave you two alone." Clive looks directly at me. "We have a meeting in twenty minutes, Rowan. I need you there. Don't be late."

I smile softly knowing that he's giving me the gift of an escape in the form of an imaginary meeting. I don't confide that often in Clive but I sense that he can read between the lines of what's happening between Caleb and me. He saw how weary I was when I got back to the office last week after seeing Caleb. "I won't be late."

I watch in silence as Clive walks through the doorway into the corridor. I don't have time to react before Caleb takes a step, slams my office door shut and turns to look at me with his hands on his hips.

"What?" I say out of pure exasperation. "What is it?"

"Where's my brother?" He taps his foot against the carpeted floor. "My brother is gone and I want to know where the hell he is."

FIFTEEN

"Asher's not gone," I say confidentially as I sit behind my desk. "What makes you think he's gone?"

He follows my lead and lowers himself into one of the chairs in front of my desk. "He hasn't been back to the office since…since I…I've tried to call him several times and he won't pick up."

I glare across the desk at me. "You fired him, Caleb. Why would he want to talk to you?"

Logic often escapes Caleb. He can't see what's directly in front of him because his mind is so twisted around what should be happening as opposed to what is really happening. "He knows that I wasn't serious."

It's another symptom of his over inflated ego. He thinks he can cut people down at their knees and within the next breath, they'll figure out that he's simply doing it to satiate a need within him for control and power. "He doesn't know that. He has no intention of coming back to work with you right now."

Irritation washes over his expression. If there's a loop to be in, Caleb definitely doesn't want to be standing outside the perimeter of that. "You know where he is, don't you? You've talked to him."

I haven't. The last conversation I had with Asher was when he told me he was considering going to see his mother. He promised me then that we'd have a chance to say goodbye before he jetted off. "I haven't talked to him in a few days."

"Look at me, Rowan." His tone is controlled and measured.

I raise my eyes until my gaze is locked with his. "What?"

"I need to talk to him about a work issue that he left hanging." He exhales audibly. "It's crucial."

My spirit deflates almost instantly. "You're not worried about him? You just want to talk to him about work?"

If my words impacted him at all, he's masking it with effortless ease. "I need to speak to my brother about work. If you know where he is, I need you to tell me."

I glance down at my smartphone. I have every confidence that if I called Asher right now, he'd pick up. He rarely ignores my calls or text messages and during the infrequent times that he has, he's called me back as soon as he could. It happened the day he was arrested and I know that he's reachable if I need him. "I have no idea where your bother iHis head bows as he considers my words. "I haven't asked much of you over the years, Row. I'm asking you now to find Asher for me if you can."

If he'd followed the plea up with any words of compassion concerning his need to know that his brother is safe and sound after being arrested, I'd be tempted to call Asher on the spot. That's not what this is. He's not looking for a way back into his brother's trust; he's looking for a colleague who holds the keys to a deal he has to close.

"I can't find him for you. I don't know where he is."

I hear his teeth tap a rhythmic beat as his jaw clenches. "You told Clive you were calling someone to make dinner plans. Who is he?"

I close my eyes and shake my head. "Don't ask me that."

"I want to know."

"Why?" My eyes pop open. "I don't ask you about the women you date. You don't need to know about the men I date."

"I'm curious," he says quietly. "I'd like to know his name. I may know the guy."

"You don't know him," I say shakily. "I can't keep doing this with you. You can't know every detail of my life."

"We're friends, Rowan." He looks down at his lap. "You're my oldest friend."

"It worked when we were kids, Caleb." I hear the anxiety that is coursing through me in my own voice. "It kind of worked when I was in college. It's not working anymore."

"What does that mean?" He scratches the back of his head. "How is it not working?"

"You exhaust me," I admit as my voice cracks. I look past his shoulder to my closed office door. I suddenly feel suffocated. "You hurt Asher. You want to know every detail of my life. You take so much. You're always taking from me and I get nothing back."

He leans his right arm on the chair's armrest. "What do you want from me, Rowan? What am I not giving to you?"

"Respect," I say clearly. "Honesty. You don't value anything I say. You knew that having Asher arrested would hurt me and you did it. You didn't think about how he'd feel or how I'd feel or anyone else."

"I was worried about telling you." His thigh shakes as he taps his foot quickly on the carpet. "I knew you'd be upset. I thought you'd understand though."

"You thought I'd tell you that you did the right thing," I correct him. "That's why you told me first and not Gabriel or your parents. You thought I'd back you up and reassure you."

"No." He shakes his head slightly. "I thought you'd see the value in what I did. I know you worry about him falling back into his old habits. I thought it would scare him if he was arrested."

"It broke him." My hands leap to my chest. "It hurt him. You're his brother. He's supposed to be able to count on you."

"I'm supposed to be able to count on him." He straightens his legs and I wonder briefly if he's going to jump to his feet. "He can't hide behind his addiction forever. It's not an excuse."

I stare at him as I try and absorb the words. "He's not like you, Caleb. He's nothing like you."

"You keep telling me that," he spits the words out through clenched teeth. "I'm sick and tired of hearing about how wonderful my fucked up brother is."

"He's not fucked up," I seethe as I slam my palm into my desk. "He's human. He's not perfect. He's just trying to make it through life. That's it."

His shoulders fall back into the chair. "You've picked your side. You actually picked his side."

I want to scream. I want to shake him until the boy I used to know floats back into view. "I chose to be a friend to Asher. That's all I've done."

He pushes himself slowly to his feet. I watch as he buttons his suit jacket and straightens his tie. "After what you went through with Tom you'd think you would have learned your lesson. I'm done trying to help either of you. If you want Asher, he's all yours and you can both stay the hell away from me and my business."

My bottom lip quivers but I don't respond as he pulls his gaze from me before he opens my office door and disappears down the bustling corridor.

SIXTEEN

"Who knew Caleb Foster was such a raging bitch?"

I have to physically push my hand into my lips to keep myself from spitting out my dinner. I turn to look at Graham. He's holding a glass of wine in one hand and a fork in the other.

"You're not actually considering talking to him again, are you?"

I shrug my shoulder while I chew quickly. "I don't know. We've argued before."

"Arguing is one thing, Rowan." His index finger flies into the air towards me. "You two didn't have an argument. He just lost it. That's an entirely different thing."

I can't disagree. It's been more than a week since Caleb stormed out of my office. I was tempted to call him the next day to smooth things over but my pride wouldn't allow it.

Instead, I'd busied myself on a new project at work and had dragged Ivy to a Broadway play and yoga class a few times. If I can keep my mind occupied, I can keep it from wandering to thoughts of Caleb.

We've gone weeks, and even months, at times without talking but we've never left things in such a difficult place before. Whenever we've argued in the past, one of us has reached out to the other within a day or two. It's not happening this time and even though part of me is in full-on panic mode over the idea of never talking to Caleb again, I can't bring myself to call him or send him a text. I know if I do, I'll be pulled back into his feud with Asher. I need to move my life forward and if that means creating distance from the Foster brothers, I'm going to stay on that path.

"I'm going to start work next week," Graham handily changes the subject and I'm grateful for the unexpected shift.

Since we've been roommates, Graham has spent most of his days sitting in the apartment, wallowing in the grief of his divorce. I haven't asked too many questions about his career goals mainly because each time I've brought up anything to do with his life before he left New

York, he immediately dives into a conversation about his marriage. He's always made certain that his part of the rent was in my hand before the first of the month, which is the only thing that really matters.

"That's great," I offer cautiously. "Where are you working?"

"Here and there." He taps his fork on the edge of the plate in front of him. "I'm actually going to be a personal assistant."

"Where?" I stop myself when I see him cock a dark brow. "Or is it who? Who are you working for?"

"Libby Duncan," he almost screams her name out as he claps his hands together. "I'm the new personal assistant to Libby Duncan."

I'm not a theatre buff. I don't line up to grab tickets when a new play or musical opens. I've been to two Broadway shows in the past six months and both of those have been with Ivy. Libby Duncan was the star of one of them and after the performance I watched as Ivy warmly embraced her. They're friends and I'm guessing that's how Graham got the upper hand in landing that sought after job.

"Ivy took me to see her in that new musical," I begin before I realize I can't remember the name of the production. "She was incredible. She's really talented."

"She's the best." He lifts his wine glass. "It's a grueling job but I'm up for the challenge considering I get to watch her perform in eight shows every week."

I can't help but smile. This is the first time I've seen any excitement on Graham's face since he moved in with me. "It sounds like it's going to be a blast."

"The job comes with a shitload of perks." He scratches his chin. "The salary is insane too."

I'm genuinely happy for him. He's been through the emotional wringer this past year and if anyone deserves to find happiness, it's Graham. "You're not going to forget about me now that you'll be hanging out with Broadway folks, will you?"

"I'm right there whenever you need me, Row." He reaches across the table to pat the top of my hand. "If you call, I'll come running."

* * *

I adjust the pillows behind my head as I try to type out a text message to Asher while I'm on my side in my bed.

I'm getting worried. Call or text. Please.

I stare at the phone for what feels like ten minutes waiting for a response. I get absolutely nothing back in return. I slide my thumb over the screen. I open the clock app and then wince when I realize the current time in Brussels. If Asher has already made his way over there, he's fast asleep at this point. Badgering him with another call or another text won't help the situation. I know that he'll call when he's ready and until then, I have to stay clear minded and focused on my life.

I close the app and open my messages back up again. I reread the one I received earlier from Tyler Monroe, the man Ivy's intent on setting me up with. It's nothing more than a cordial greeting asking how I am. I start to type a response before I delete it.

My heart may be ready to venture out into the world again, but my mind isn't. I'm too tired to start up a text conversation with a potential date. I need rest and the only way I'm going to find that is if I shut off my mind, put my phone on the bedside table and drift off into a deep sleep.

SEVENTEEN

I'm startled awake by a series of loud thumps. I reach for my phone wondering if I somehow managed to change the ring tone on it again. I scan the screen and see absolutely nothing other than that it's barely past seven in the morning.

It's Saturday. I don't jump from my bed as soon as the sun rises once the weekend arrives. I take my time getting my day started. I lounge in bed, sometimes reading the news on my tablet before I even think about what I want to have for breakfast. If I make it into the shower by noon, I know I'm on track for a good day. If I've had a bad week, I may hide between my sheets for the entire day, ordering in food and watching movies. Today, I need to stop by the office, so I should be thanking whatever the hell that noise was that jarred me from my dreams of a tropical island and a shirtless man bringing me an endless supply of petty drinks with umbrellas.

The thumps are there again and I realize they're coming from my apartment door. I close my eyes hoping that Graham heard it first and he's at the door, chasing away whoever thinks it's acceptable to bang on a door this early in the day.

He's not and the next louder, and more persistence, knocks are proof of that. I pull a white tank top over my head and a slip into a pair of white lace panties. I have no intention of opening the door. It's thin enough that I can carry on a conversation with whoever is on the other side. All I really need to do is tell them to scram. I'm still sleepy and craving the comfort of my bed, so I'm going to make short work of this distraction.

"What is it?" I call through the crack between the door and the doorjamb. "Who is there?"

"It's me." His voice is low and quiet. "Open the door."

I peer through the cracked glass peek hole in the door. It's Caleb. His hands are resting on the door. His shirt is a wrinkled mess and he hasn't shaved in days. He looks like hell. My hand hovers over the doorknob.

"What do you want, Caleb?" I volley back hoping that I won't have to talk face-to-face to him right now. "You woke me up."

"Bell." His voice cracks slightly. "God, I need to talk to you. Please just open it."

My breath catches at the sound of my nickname. I haven't heard it flow from his lips in years. I doubt that his voice had even gone through its adolescent change when he last said it. My lips quiver as I answer back. "What's wrong?"

"Open the door." He taps his hand softly against the wood. "Open the fucking door. Please, just do it."

I reach down and twist the deadbolt lock so it pops open. I grasp the door handle before I turn it, pulling the door open.

I have no time to react before he slides into my apartment, yanks me into his arms and pulls me tightly into his chest.

"Caleb," I whisper into the fabric of his blue dress shirt. "What? What is it?"

He doesn't answer. His body only jerks slightly as he works to control his emotions. I try to break free to look at his face but he molds my body into his.

"Just tell me," I say calmly even though my heart is racing. "I can help if you tell me."

His body tenses slightly before he grabs my shoulders and pushes himself back. I close my eyes briefly before I look up into his.

"Bell." His voice lowers as he brushes his lips against my forehead. "Christ, please."

"What?" My bottom lip trembles. "Just say it."

"It's Asher." His eyes fill with tears. "I'm so sorry."

A slow realization pours through me and I feel one solitary tear fall down my cheek. "What about him? He's in Brussels with your mom. He told me he was going there."

"No," he says through a sob.

"No?" I try to break free of his grasp. I pull him forward just as reaches back to slam my apartment door closed with his foot.

"He's not in Brussels." His grip tightens on my arm. "He never went there. I've been trying to find him for days."

"Where is he?" I point towards the window. "We can go find him."

"We can't." His hand leaves my shoulder and jumps to his chest. "He's gone, Bell."

"No," I say louder. "He's not. Don't say that."

"It's the truth." He swallows hard as he says the words. "They found a body this morning in a hotel on the lower East Side. There were drugs in the room."

"No," I scream the word so loud that it bounces off the walls of the almost barren apartment. "No."

"I have to go identify him." His eyes close. "I need you to come with me. Please, Rowan, come with me."

I lean forward to rest my head on his chin as I nod slowly. "I'll go. I know it's not him. Asher wouldn't do this to us. You'll see."

EIGHTEEN

We haven't spoken a word to each other since we left the morgue. We also haven't let go of one another's hands since the stretcher with the body was brought towards us. When the woman in charge pulled down the sheet, Caleb had gasped. I'd stood next to him stoic and silent.

"I don't want to go home," he says as much to me as to the driver of the car. He'd called one of the company's drivers into action when the police had called him. "Take us back to Rowan's apartment."

My eyes fall to my lap to where our hands are still tightly woven together. I'm grateful that he's not dumping me back at my place before he goes to shelter himself in his own apartment.

I hold tight to his hand when the driver opens the back door of the car. I allow Caleb to help me out and I lean into his body as we move silently through the lobby of my building and into the elevator.

"Can I stay all day?" The words come out in a low growl. "I want to stay all day."

I nod against his chest, closing my eyes briefly to try to find the strength I'll need to walk from the bank of elevators to my apartment door.

"Is your roommate home?" He fumbles with my keys as we step off the lift.

I pull on the sleeve of his shirt, wanting him to raise his arm. He acquiesces and I twist it around so I can look at the watch. "He meets a friend for coffee on Saturday mornings. He's gone by now."

He opens the door before pushing it open. He holds my hand as he pulls me inside.

"Do you want some coffee?" I glance towards the small galley kitchen. "We have coffee. I can make some."

"I want to go to bed." He finally drops my hand as his fingers fly to the buttons of his shirt. "I need to close my eyes."

I nod silently as I turn towards the hallway. "You can rest in my bed. I'll show you."

"Come with me, Bell." He wraps his arm around my waist. "Lay with me."

I don't respond. I rest my hands over his arm, step forward and lead him into my bedroom before I shut the door behind us.

* * *

"I fell asleep." His breath is against my cheek. "How long have I been sleeping?"

I glance at my phone. I've been holding tightly to it since I laid next to Caleb after he slid his shirt from his shoulders and fell into my bed. I'd watched the gentle rise and fall of his chest as he drifted off to sleep. I listened to the soft sound of his snoring when he turned towards me and I'd cupped my hand over his cheek when he mumbled something I couldn't quite understand. "It's been about three hours."

"You haven't slept." He nods towards my phone. "Have you been on that since we got here?"

"No." I twist around so I can rest it on the edge of my bedside table. "I was just texting my friend. I was supposed to meet her for lunch today."

Normally he'd be shooting off questions about who I'm meeting and where. "I feel numb, Rowan. I feel numb inside."

I shift my body until my head is resting back on my pillow. I pull on the bottom of the sweatshirt I'd put on before we'd left my apartment this morning. Caleb had barely given me enough time to yank on a pair of jeans and rummage for a shirt before he'd pulled me into the hallway.

"You were so strong today." He brushes a piece of my hair from my forehead. "How did you get to be so strong?"

"I'm not strong." I smile softly. "I just knew it wasn't him."

He looks directly into my eyes. "You didn't believe it was him for a minute, did you?"

I fist my hand to keep from reaching up to cup his cheek again. It felt natural and comfortable when I did it when he was fast asleep. Now that he's awake and he's staring right at me, I feel vulnerable and exposed. "I'm not sure. Maybe I just didn't want to believe it was him."

"I filed a missing person's report two days ago." He swallows hard. "I've contacted everyone I can think of who might know where he is. No one has seen him in weeks."

I lick my lips. "I've tried to contact him too but he doesn't answer. It's not like him to go silent on me."

"You care about him a lot, don't you?" He raises a brow. Normally when Caleb would ask me that question, my defenses would kick into high gear. I know that he feels threatened by the closeness of my friendship with his brother. It has to stem from the sibling rivalry that has always been a part of the dynamic between the three brothers.

"He's my friend, Caleb," I answer without hesitation. "I can't imagine my life without him."

He shifts slightly on the bed. His lips move but he doesn't say anything. I can tell from the expression on his face that there's a question right there, sitting on the tip of his tongue.

"What?" I ask softly. "What is it?"

"It's just..." he stops as he leans closer to me. "It's just that I think about you a lot. I think about when we were kids."

Out of a sheer need to breathe, I slide away from him until I'm on my back again. "What do you think about? When you would pull those pranks on me and my friends?"

His eyes light up in the warm afternoon sun that is pouring in through the open window. "You always screamed when I scared you on Halloween."

"That's because you'd wait by the side of the stoop with a mask on and jump out at me when I came outside." I tap him playfully on his bare chest.

He shifts and moves one of his arms around me until he's hovering directly above me. "I loved scaring you then. I don't want to scare you now."

"You don't scare me, Caleb." I stare at his lips. "I'm not scared of you."

Time feels as though it stalls as he tilts his head slightly to the side before he lowers it. I catch my breath when his soft, full lips finally touch mine for the very first time.

NINETEEN

The urgency of his kiss increases as his hand leaps to my chin. He holds my head exactly where he wants it as he pushes my lips apart with his tongue. I moan into the kiss. The sound only spurs him on more and he bites my bottom lip softly.

I reach up to grab his shoulders. One of my hands slides to the back of his neck and with that a low growl pours from within him and into me.

I whimper from everything I feel. I can't control it. I may not have admitted it to myself or anyone else, but I've wanted this since I knew what kissing was. I've dreamt of what his lips and breath would taste like. I've compared every man I've ever been with to Caleb even though I've never touched him in an intimate way.

He pushes his body into mine and I instantly feel his erection beneath his pants. He's as aroused as I am. I want this. I'm wet just from the taste of his kiss.

His hand drops to my leg and without thinking I arch my hips off the b"Rowan," he whispers against my lips. "Yes."

I pull him back into the kiss. My tongue sliding against his in a sensual invitation to give me everything his body has to offer. He pulls back abruptly. It's so fast that I actually moan into the silent air.

His hand finds the bottom of the sweatshirt and he pushes it up and over my head. I struggle to rid myself of it but once I do I toss it next to us on the bed. All I'm wearing is the thin, white tank top I had put on when he woke me earlier.

I watch silently as his eyes travel over the front of the shirt. My nipples are hard, swollen and straining against the flimsy material. His hands fall to my waist as his eyes meet mine. I see the same hunger within them that I feel.

"You're so beautiful." His right hand slides over my body towards my breast. "I can't believe how beautiful you are."

I push my face into the pillow wanting to absorb everything I'm hearing and feeling. I gasp loudly when I feel his teeth gently tug at my nipple through the shirt. My hand leaps to the back of his head, wanting to feel more. I'm desperate to steal every possible sensation I came from this.

In one swift and gentle movement, his hand is sliding down my body and beneath the waistband of my pants. I can't control the whimper that escapes me when he edges his hand under the lace of my panties and I moan loudly when his fingers run through my soft, moist folds until they settle on my clit.

"You're so wet." He pushes my legs apart with one of his. "I knew you'd feel so good."

I try to control my desperate need to come beneath his touch but it's futile. He's circling my clit with expert strokes, applying just enough pressure to bring me closer to the edge.

"I've thought about what your body looks like, Bell." He breathes the words into the air between us. "I've thought about the sounds you make when you come."

The words only make me more desirous. I cover my face with my hand, suddenly feeling incredibly exposed.

"No." He shakes his head. "Let me see. Let me watch."

I drop my hand slowly to my chest as I allow the pleasure to run through my body. I push my wetness into his hand, wanting to feel even more.

"You're getting close." He lowers his mouth to my nipple and sucks it through the thin material. "I've wanted this for so long."

I close my eyes as I feel the heat racing through me. I bite my bottom lip to quiet the raging need I have to scream his name and just when he pulls back to look at me, I lock eyes with him as I fall over the edge into an intense orgasm.

"That's it," his voice is a low growl. "Come for me, Row. Come for me."

I whimper as I try to move away from his hand but he doesn't stop. He only presses harder, stimulating me more as he slides a finger into my channel and pushes me towards another release.

"Caleb," I say his name without realizing it. "Caleb."

"I've never seen anything as beautiful as you." His lips are on mine again. His kiss hot and wanting. His tongue is lush and soft as it glides into my mouth.

I cry out as the climax bears down on me just as I hear the sharp shrill ring of a smartphone bite through the air.

TWENTY

Ten minutes later, I'm standing in the shower, the hot water beating a path over my tender flesh. I still feel as though my core is on fire. I've come with men before but it's never been that intense. I know that logically it's not just the sensations that my body was feeling. It has much more to do with the tangled emotions that I feel for Caleb. I've had fantasies for years about the touch of his skin and the taste of him and now that I've felt the skill in his hands and breathed in the heady scent of him, I want him even more.

He'd ignored the phone the first time it rang. After I came, he'd kissed me tenderly while I fumbled with the belt of his pants. I'd wanted to slide down the bed and take him in my mouth. I wanted to give him pleasure in the way I've always imagined I would. In my wildest and most arousing dreams, Caleb is standing against a wall, while I'm on my knees, and his hands are on my head. His cock is sliding in and out of my mouth and his breath is labored and heavy as he comes hard and gives me a taste of everything that he is.

I'd nodded in patient agreement when he told me that he had to take the call and I'd finally rolled off the bed and slid into the bathroom when he stood up, turned his back to me and walked to the window to talk about an order of shirts that hadn't been shipped.

The bite of rejection is there, albeit not as harsh as it might be if I hadn't stopped before leaving the room to look back to see him staring at me. His hand had leapt to his chest and he'd closed his eyes. It was a gesture that was born on the playground when he was in the sixth grade and I was in the first. I was scared and unsure during those first days of school and he had told me that he'd always be there and I would know that if I looked for him in the corridors and saw him holding his heart.

I turn off the water when I feel it shift from hot to warm. It may be the middle of the afternoon on a Saturday but showers in this building are best served short. I've brought up the issue of the lack of hot water to the super only to be told that there's nothing he can do about it and water conservation is a good cause to support.

I towel off quickly before tugging a comb through my damp hair. I pull on Graham's blue patterned robe because mine is still buried in one of the boxes I brought with me when I moved out of the apartment I shared with Tom. I've always claimed laziness as a reason for not unpacking everything. My brother would argue that point in favor of my holding out hope that Tom and I will eventually reconcile. Unless I'm willing to throw my entire life away for a quick high, I will never be with Tom again.

A quiet knock on the door shakes me from my thoughts. I glide my hand over the steam covered mirror to look at my reflection before I turn to the left to yank open the door.

"I'm sorry about the call." He's dressed now. His shirt and tie are both back in place, his suit jacket hanging over his arm. "I need to go into the office."

I should point out that it's Saturday and that we were in the middle of something, but he knows those things. They're obvious and undeniable. I doubt that he knows that his running off is making me feel used.

I nod. "Is it a big problem?"

"It could wait until Monday," he begins before he furrows his brow. "I mean, I like to take care of problems immediately so there's no break in production."

I pull the robe closed tightly over my chest. "I understand."

"I'm not running away from what happened…I'm trying to say that I like what happened in your room, Rowan." He closes his eyes briefly. "We were both really emotional this morning. I was scared about Asher."

"Me too," I say through a sigh. "I'm relieved it wasn't him."

"I'll hire someone to find him." He shuffles his feet against the weathered cork floor. "I'll do that today."

I'm grateful that he's taking that step. I should express that but I don't want to cloud the moment with words of gratitude that may be construed as being about what happened earlier. I'm not going to thank him for getting me off when he's intent on racing out the door to save a shipment of shirts.

"I'll call you soon." He leans forward and brushes his lips over my cheek before he turns on his heel and walks out of my apartment.

TWENTY-ONE

"Maybe his dick is hideous."

Again, the food in my mouth almost flies out mid laugh. I have to stop chewing in order to avoid swallowing because I know I'll choke. I turn to the left to see a huge grin on Graham's face.

"I bet that's what it is," Ivy agrees almost instantly. "My first lover, Mark, had a really ugly penis. It was shaped like a…"

"Stop," I say loudly as I dart my hand into the air. "I'm not going to have a discussion about cocks in the middle of this restaurant. I happen to like coming to Axel NY. I don't want to get thrown out."

"I know the owner." Ivy searches the room. "He won't care if we talk about it."

"I care," I point out. "You two can talk about it all you want once I leave. I can't stay for dessert."

Graham juts out his bottom lip into a pout. "You can't leave. We're here for you. Ivy and I are going to help you get through this."

"I'm fine," I half-lie as I pick at the salad on my plate.

"You're not fine." Ivy motions towards our server. "You need more wine."

I shake my head as I hold my hand over the top of my glass. "I don't need anymore. One glass is my limit."

"I know you're upset, Rowan." Graham taps my shoulder. "I saw how you looked when I got home on Saturday."

I wish Graham hadn't marched through the door less than fifteen minutes after Caleb left. The emotional weight of the day had gotten to me and I was sitting in the living room, crying my eyes out. Most of that was genuine relief over the fact that Asher was just missing, and not dead. The other part, which is the part I expressed to Graham, was that I felt a definite shift in Caleb when the phone rang and he tore himself away from me.

I know the Fosters' business from listening to Caleb talk about it for years. I understand that both Caleb and Gabriel have a work ethic that is impressive. I also know that Caleb could have delegated the issue to someone else. He could have made a call and solved the problem in an instant. He didn't do that. Instead, he chose to walk away with little explanation.

"It's not the first time I've been rejected by a man. It won't be the last. I'll talk to Caleb about it so we can clear the air."

"How exactly do you talk to a guy about something like this?" Ivy asks as she waves at someone across the room. "I mean it happened a couple of times with me and Jax but he realized right away and dropped whatever he was doing to focus on me."

Thanks for pointing out yet again how utterly perfect your husband is, Ivy.

"Caleb and I can talk about anything." I smile when I see the owner of the restaurant, Hunter Reynolds, walking towards us. "I'll just be direct. We will clear the air and everything will go back to the way it used to be."

"It will never be the way it used to be." Graham leans close to whisper the words into my ear. "Your friendship with Caleb is ruined. He crossed a line. You two can't go back."

I don't glance in his direction. I absorb his words knowing that he's right. What Caleb and

I did in my apartment changed the path of our friendship forever.

"Rowan Bell," Hunter Reynolds says my name as he extends his hand out towards me. "I'm glad to finally meet you."

"I'm glad to meet you too," I parrot back as I smile and pretend that I'm having the time of my life in his restaurant even though my heart is breaking inside.

* * *

I scrub my hands over my face as the taxi weaves a path through the streets of Manhattan. I know that I should be going to see Caleb. The smart and sane thing to do would be to confront him now and clear the air.

We haven't spoken at all in the three days since he left my apartment in a hurry. I have no sense of what's happening with Asher even though I've continually tried to contact him. I did try to follow up with the police detective assigned to investigate the missing person's report Caleb filed but he was reluctant to share anything given that I'm not a member of the Foster family. My last approach is to contact Gabriel. He's due back in New York in two days but I know him and I know that he'll be livid once he learns that Asher is missing.

"Here is good?" The taxi driver pulls the car to a stop in front of my building.

"Here is good." I rifle through my wallet for a few bills.

I hear him telling me to have a good night as I step out of the car and onto the street. I slam the car door shut and watch him take off in search of another fare before I finally turn towards my building and the sight of Caleb Foster leaning against the brick façade.

TWENTY-TWO

"I don't have a lot of friends, Rowan," he says as I hand him a bottle of water. "You might be my only friend."

"You have your brothers," I point out before I realize how ironic that statement is given the fact that Gabriel is half a world away and Asher is missing.

He pulls the cap from the bottle before he takes a heavy swallow. "I can't remember a time when you weren't my friend."

I ease into the chair that's across from him. I knew, before we entered the apartment, that we'd be alone. I'd left Graham and Ivy at the restaurant with Hunter to enjoy a lavish dessert treat. Judging by the way the three of them were getting along, I don't expect to see Graham for at least a few hours.

"I told Gabriel about Asher." He skims his hand over the leg of his jeans. "He's putting on a brave face."

"What about your parents?"

"Mom is worried." He dips his chin towards the floor. "Dad made a comment about Asher being a disgrace."

I shake my head disgusted by Roman Foster's reaction to his son's ongoing issues with addiction. "Your dad is something else."

"He lives in his own world." He cradles the bottle in his palm as he leans back in the chair, crossing his legs. "I can't change that."

It's a surprisingly mature outlook coming from the man who typically launches into a tirade the moment anyone disagrees with his stance.

"What about the person you hired to find Asher?" It's the question that has been eating at me since I saw Caleb on the street outside. "Is there any news about where he is?"

"He hasn't used his passport or credit cards." He taps his finger on the cap of the bottle. "Gabriel thinks he might be at one of the properties the company owns."

It's wishful thinking at best but if there's hope I'm going to be the first one to stand in line to grab hold of it.

"Will someone check on those places?" I ask even though it's obvious that if it hasn't already been done, it will be soon.

"We're arranging that now."

"Good." I shift on the chair I'm sitting in. "Is there anything else? The detective didn't find anything else?"

"Nothing yet," he counters. "He was asking about what happened the last time I saw Asher."

I know that it's very likely that the last time Caleb saw his brother it was in my office when the two of them stared each other down before Caleb took his leave. "What did you tell him?"

"I told him about Asher lashing out." He inches forward in his chair. "He wanted to know if there was anything else. Did he say anything to you before he disappeared?"

I scratch the side of my nose. This is one of those situations where you can't win for losing. I've kept quiet, up to this point, about Asher telling me that something had upset him the morning he was arrested. I know that I should have mentioned it to Caleb sooner but it's not as if I have a looking glass pointed towards where Asher has hidden himself away from the world. "He said something to me."

His face is emotionless. "My brother said something to you before he disappeared?"

I hear the sound of the plastic bend as he fists his hand around the half-empty bottle of water. I look him straight in the eye as I respond. "He went to see someone that morning. It was the morning he was arrested."

"Who did he go see?"

I rub both hands over my face. "I don't know. He just said that he had an appointment before work and that he got news that upset him."

"That's it? That's all he said?"

"That's it," I say quietly.

"You didn't think to mention this sooner?" he asks tightly. "You didn't think that it might be worthwhile to tell me that my brother got bad news the day he flipped out?"

I feel indignation course through me. I want to stop him on the spot to point out that before Asher disappeared into thin air, Caleb didn't give a shit about what was happening with him. "I didn't know any of the details."

"Did he tell you not to tell me? Is that what happened? You made a promise to each other again and you can't break it?"

The sarcasm dripping off the words is palpable and thick. "He told me he was upset after an appointment. That's all I know."

"You know where he is, don't you?" He points his index finger right at me.

Even though I recognize his anger talking, I won't dive into that with him. I don't want to argue about Asher. "I have no idea where he is."

"That's why you were so calm when we went to the morgue." His eyes close as he pushes his head back into the leather chair. "You didn't bat a fucking eyelash because you knew he was fine."

I bite my lip to stop the flood of emotions that tear through me. "I wouldn't do that to you. I would never keep that information from you."

"Tell me where he is." He rests his elbows on his knees. "Just tell me."

"I don't know," I say clearly and slowly. "I have no idea where Asher is."

"I need to talk to him." His gaze narrows. "If you have access to him, now is the time to tell me."

"I don't," I spit back.

"I came here to talk about what happened." He points towards the hallway. "That was a mistake, Rowan. I don't know what I was thinking."

That you wanted me? That you ached to be inside of me? That the pull that has been there between us for years is real?

"You're sorry that it happened?" I ask for blunt clarification. Now isn't the time to skim around the edges of this. I want a clear and concrete answer about how he feels.

"It should never have happened." He's on his feet before I have time to react. "We're friends. We almost lost that. I can't risk damaging what we already have. I need you as a friend. I'll always need you as a friend."

I don't look up. I know that if I do he'll catch a glimpse of the disappointment that's washed over me. "We'll never do it again."

"We can't," he says quietly as he turns on his heel. "I need to go but if you hear from my brother, call me…or…you can call Gabriel. Just let one of us know."

TWENTY-THREE

"I need someone to go to Martha's Vineyard for me." Clive is standing in the doorway of my office. "If you tell me you're sending Jordan, I'm going to need to remind you that she just got back from Dallas a few weeks ago with her husband in tow. She's still refreshed."

I smile faintly at the joke. "What's in Martha's Vineyard?"

"There's a very smart developer there who has come up with a software program that I want the rights to." He takes a heavy step into my office. "He hates New York so we need to go to him to get the deal done."

"Imogen can handle it," I point out. "She loves it up there."

"Imogen has court on Friday." He doesn't miss a beat with his retort. "I'm suing a competitor so she's focused on that. She's drawn up the documents for the sale of the rights of the software so you just need to fly there, get them signed and fly back."

I always refer trips like this to Imogen Ford, the legal expert at Corteck. She's constantly asking either Clive or me if there's any way she can get out of the office for a few days. It's actually the perfect getaway for her. "She can't switch her court date? Can't you sue whoever you're suing this week another time?"

"You're not funny," he mutters under his breath. "The trip will be a good distraction for you. I know that Caleb's brother is still missing."

It's a thought that never escapes me. I think about it the moment I open my eyes in the morning and it's the last thought that drifts across my mind before I close my eyes at night. I panic at times, like I did this morning when I was in the shower, but I have to trust in Asher. He wouldn't hurt himself or put himself in peril. He's worked too hard these past few months to piece his life back together. Throwing that all away just to chase a fleeting high doesn't make sense to me. I may be foolish to believe that he's changed as much as I hope he has but the alternative is to sit and fret over his safety. I can't do that. I'll drive myself to the brink of insanity if I do.

"I need to be there on Friday?"

"You can fly in on Friday morning and be on your way back to solid ground within a couple of hours." He nods in the direction of my laptop. "I'll email you all the details."

I absolutely hate the thought of leaving New York right now with the weight of Asher's disappearance hanging over my head but I know that the time away will do me good. It's a change of scenery and it's also an escape from the gnawing ache I feel inside over what happened between Caleb and me. "I'll take care of it."

"I knew you would, Rowan." He tosses me a wide grin. "You never let me dow

* * *

"I let Asher down." Gabriel embraces me the moment I step off the private elevator and into his penthouse. It's been months since I've seen the eldest Foster brother. He hasn't changed at all. He's still as devastatingly handsome as I remember him.

"No." I push my hands into his. "Asher has always talked about how much you've done for him. He looks up to you."

"Listen to you." He steps back slightly. "You're the voice of reason."

Hearing the words from Gabriel brings me comfort and serenity. He's the calmest and most centered of the clan. He's thirty-two now and the man I see standing before me is just an older version of the boy who used to sit on my stoop telling me about the different constellations in the night sky. He's always been studious, reserved and brilliant. "I'm the voice of hope."

"That you are." He drops my hands as he turns towards the open space. "Do you want something, Rowan? I have some coffee made or I can whip up a cocktail."

I'm tempted to ask him for a Cosmopolitan. It's been an incredibly long day and the only bright spot was the knowledge that I'd be standing in his apartment looking at him. "I'm fine. I don't need anything."

"You'll sit." He waves his hand towards a long leather couch. "You'll tell me about what's going on. I tried to talk to Caleb but he's all over the place."

That's an understatement. Caleb had texted me earlier asking if I could talk to his private detective tomorrow morning. I shot him a quick text back explaining that I had to head out of town. I hadn't gotten a reply and at this point, I'm grateful that our correspondence is at a bare minimum. I'm still feeling a rush of confusion about the day we kissed in my apartment.

"Asher was arrested," I begin knowing that Gabriel may not have heard about that. It's doubtful that Caleb would tell his older brother about what happened in the office that day. "It happened at the corporate office."

"Asher told me." Gabriel arches his head back to look up at the high ceilings. "He called me a few days after that."

I had no idea. "How was he when you spoke to him?"

"He was frustrated with Caleb," he starts before he pulls his gaze back to me. "I'm frustrated with him too."

"Me too," I mumble under my breath. Beyond telling Graham and Ivy, I haven't shared the details of what happened between Caleb and me last week with anyone.

"Where do you think he is, Rowan?" He twists in his seat to look back at the bank of windows that overlook Central Park. "Do you think he's still in New York? I want to find him. I need to."

TWENTY-FOUR

"If I had any idea, I'd tell you Gabriel," I assure him as I stand to walk towards the windows. "I've spent hours thinking about where he could be. I walk past the brownstone your family used to live in every day hoping he's there, sitting on the stoop the way he used to do when we were kids."

A small grin tugs at the corner of his lips. "He loved that house. When he was in rehab he talked about buying it one day. He wants to raise his kids in that neighborhood."

I turn to smile at him. For the first time, since Asher disappeared I feel actual hope. Gabriel speaks about him as if he's returning. He has the same faith in his brother that I do.

"It's a great place to raise a family."

"It is, "I agree quietly. "Asher will be an amazing dad."

"He wants that. He talks about it or he did when he was still here."

I close my eyes to ward off the emotional tidal wave I feel bearing down on me. "We need to find him."

"We're going to find him." He stands behind me, his hands resting on my shoulders. "I'm back and I'm not giving up until my little brother is home safe and sound."

"If I can do anything to help, you'll let me know, right?"

"You've been holding down the fort since I've been gone." He pats my shoulder. "Caleb told me that you've been helpful."

Helpful? That's it?

"Caleb likes doing things on his own," I try to sound as non-judgemental as I can. "He hasn't asked me for much help with finding Asher."

"He told me about the morgue." I see his reflection in the glass windows as his gaze falls to the floor. "He told me you were stronger than he was that morning."

I spin around to look directly at him. "I wasn't being strong. That's not what it was. I knew it wasn't Asher. I could feel it inside. I think I'd know if anything happened to him."

His mouth thins. "The last time I spoke to Asher he told me that he was feeling down. He said that life had become complicated and I warned him about using again. I specifically asked him if he was feeling the draw towards it."

"What did he say?"

"He said that he'd never do it again." He shakes his head. "He was adamant about it. I know, from the time I spent in therapy with him, that addicts will say just about anything to convince everyone they're fine."

I know that too. Tom did the very same thing when I started asking too many questions. He'd rush out to buy me flowers and he'd take me to my favorite restaurant all while telling me that he'd never use anything illicit again. I believed him because I was the one who needed to hear those words, even if my logical mind was telling me that they weren't true.

"I can tell when Asher is lying to me." He blinks, and then looks directly at me. "He wasn't lying when he promised me he wouldn't break his sobriety."

"I believe that too," I say as I turn to look back out the window. "Asher is out there somewhere. We just have to find him."

***

"We still have that house in the Hamptons." Gabriel walks towards an oak cabinet situated on the far side of the room. "My parents never split it up in the divorce. No one has been there in years but I remember how much you loved going there when you were a kid."

I did love it. It was the highlight of my summer. My brother and I would hop in the Fosters' car with them and travel to their beautiful home in the Hamptons. We'd spend three glorious weeks there, feeling as though we'd both won the lottery. We were treated to boat rides, swimming, tennis and all the personal chef prepared food we could stomach. I always felt like a Princess when we arrived and I'd feel a terrible sense of loss once the vacation was over and we returned home.

"I haven't thought about that house in years. You never go there?"

He pulls open one of the drawers on the cabinet. His hand dips inside. "I don't have time. You should stop there on your way back from Martha's Vineyard. It's close."

"No." I shake my head wishing I hadn't mentioned my brief work trip when we spoke on the phone last night. "It would feel strange to go there after all this time."

He dangles a set of keys between his fingers. "It would give you a break from everything that's been going on here. Take the keys, Rowan. If you feel like stopping there tomorrow, do it."

I stare at the key fob. "I'll take them but I doubt I'll go there. I want to get back to help you and Caleb find Asher."

"I'm not sure how much help Caleb is going to be." His voice cracks. "I called him an hour ago and he was in a meeting. He brushed me off."

"Was it about shirts?" I ask half-jokingly.

"Shirts?" He scowls. "No. Caleb hasn't been in the office in more than a week."

"What?"

"I had a mess to clean up when I got back." He motions towards the door. "I need to go back to the office tonight."

"What's Caleb been doing? Where has he been?"

"I have no idea." He pushes the keys to the Hamptons house into my palm as he scoops up another set. "I'll ride down in the elevator with you. I'll call you as soon as I know anything."

TWENTY-FIVE

"I said that I'm here to see Caleb." I push past Ruby who is surprisingly weak considering she looks like a miniature football player in expensive heels.

"He's busy, Rhonda." Her hand leaps to my shoulder. "If you'll wait in the foyer, I'll see if he has a minute for you."

"It's Rowan." I spin back on my heel to pronounce my name slowly. "I'm going to find him. I know he's here."

I actually don't know that. It's more of an assumption than anything. I'd tried texting Caleb twice but I'd gotten no response and then I'd called. It rang at least seven times before it hit voicemail, which tells me that he didn't even glance at the screen. I've called him before when he's been consumed with work and each of those times, he's hit the ignore button in short order. This time is different.

"You can't just walk through his apartment."

"Yes, I can," I spit back defiantly. "You need to let go of my arm now."

Her eyes dart to the closed door of the library. Each time I see that door I have to chuckle to myself. Caleb may like to collect old books to display on the shelves, but he never reads them. Typically when I stop by, I'll scoop up a few to take home to read in bed. I always bring them back. I've teased him more than once about that room being my own personal library.

"Thanks for the heads-up." I nod in her direction as I swing open the heavy wooden double doors.

"Rowan?" Caleb catches sight of me the moment I step into the room. "What the hell are you doing here?"

I should take offense at the greeting. I won't though. I've caught him in the middle of something. I can tell by the panicked look on his face. I've never been a 'gotcha' type of woman. Caleb owes me nothing but the woman standing next to him looks guilty as hell. The moment my eyes rake over her I see why. The brilliant and very large diamond ring on her left hand speaks of a commitment that should be keeping her from standing alone in rooms with an incredibly handsome, and sexually insatiable, single man. "I need to talk to you, Caleb."

"What is it? What's wrong?"

I take in the muted fear in his tone as my eyes scan the room before they settle on a framed photograph. It's black and white and sitting atop a table. I stare at it, soaking in its meaning and value to him. It has to be important for him to display it out in the open like this. I instantly wonder why I've never seen it before.

"Rowan? Are you okay? What's happened?"

I pull my gaze up to meet his just as my eyes fill with tears. "Caleb," I whisper his name softly.

"Get out, Sonia," he says harshly as his eyes lock on mine. "Leave."

I take a step to the side wanting to cower away from his anger.

"Caleb, I…" the woman starts to speak. "I don't understand."

"You need to leave now." He's calm and completely in control. "You have to go."

I don't break his gaze as I sense movement beside me. I listen to her footsteps as she walks briskly out of the library closing the doors behind her.

"Tell me what's wrong?" His hand leaps to my chin. "Tell me why you're upset."

I shift my body to the right, look past his shoulder and focus on the picture of Caleb and me on the day I graduated from high school. He's staring at me, I'm smiling into the camera and there's absolutely no denying the raw emotion on both of our faces.

"You have a picture of us." I nod towards the table.

He turns quickly to grab a look before he rubs both his hands over his face. "It was an important day. I wanted a remembrance."

"Why were you there?" It's a question I've never asked before. The day was jubilant and filled with raucous celebration. I'd graduated at the top of my senior class. I'd been accepted to the college of my choice and I was dating the captain of the debate team. The fact that Caleb had come home from college to witness my graduation didn't hit me until right this very minute. "Why were you there?"

He pulls on the collar of the dark sweater he's wearing. "Our families were close, Bell. I wanted to support you."

"You were the only Foster there." I glance at the picture again. "No one else came. Only you."

"They wanted to come," he says sheepishly. "They all wanted to be there but they were busy."

Even Asher, who I saw on an almost daily basis back then, had made other plans. "You came though. I didn't come to your graduation."

He stares at me. His eyes briefly fall to the floor before they level back on my face. "I came because I had to. I came because there is no one on this earth who matters more to me than you."

TWENTY-SIX

The words he just spoke should only hold one meaning. If you've kissed a man and he's brought you intense pleasure with the gentle stroke of his fingers, you want those words to mean that he aches to be with you. You want them to capture the essence of what is in his heart. I want Caleb Foster to love me. I've always wanted that. Right now, listening to him tell me that I matter more to him than anyone else, I want that to translate to him pushing me against the wall, kissing me until my breath falls into him and making love to me in a way that binds us together forever.

"I was proud of you." His head tilts to the side as he studies my face. "I'm still proud of you. You're killing it over at Corteck."

I bite my bottom lip to quiet the urge to push him more about how much I matter to him. "I like my job. Clive is good to me."

"When you went after a business degree I thought you'd come work for us." He shifts on his feet as he gazes back at the photograph of the two of us. "It's always felt like you're part of the family. It didn't make sense when you went to work for him."

It didn't make immediate sense to me either. Foster Enterprises is an umbrella company that houses many divisions. The fashion brands are just two of their endeavors. They have a new lingerie brand, a blossoming home accessory line and they're moving into the app business. I would fit in perfectly there save for the fact that my friendship with the brothers would inevitably suffer if we all worked together. The destruction within their family is proof enough of that.

"I wanted to make it on my own. I needed to make it on my own." I cross my arms over my chest in a defiant gesture. "My career success is because of me and no one else."

He wrings his hands together. "Mine is because of my family. Everything I have I owe to them."

"You work hard," I offer because I know it's a fact. Caleb normally puts more hours in at the office than even I do, which says a lot.

"Your parents put the wheels in motion. You and your brothers took the business to the next level."

"Gabriel and I did," he subtly corrects me. "I don't think it was ever Asher's thing. He loved his music. We didn't support him in that."

Asher has been writing music since we were teenagers. I'd sometimes hear the soft sounds of his guitar floating through the open window of his bedroom and into mine during the warm months of the year. I'd often lie in my bed at night, with the gentle wind whipping my sheer curtains about while I drifted off listening to Asher's raspy voice singing the songs he'd written.

"He loves his music." I rub my fingers over my brow. "Maybe once he gets back, he can focus on that more."

"You have no doubt at all that he'll be back, do you?" His eyes plead with me to confirm that even though his voice is steady and unwavering.

"I trust that he'll find his way back here."

"I'm worried." He crosses his arms over his chest before reaching up to run his hand over his chin. "I'm worried I won't get another chance to make things right with him."

"Asher knows you love him." I take a step closer to him.

"He has secrets." His hands fall to his sides. "His life is filled with secrets."

"What?" I ask softly as a shiver runs through me. I don't want him to tell me that Asher has started using drugs again. I can't shoulder that right now after marching around for days telling everyone that he'd never use again. "What secrets?"

"That woman that just left," he begins as he looks towards the closed door of the library. "That woman knows Asher."

I push myself back to the moment when I first barged into the library. I was too focused on asking Caleb what he'd been doing that I hadn't paid any attention to the woman other than the fact that she was obviously engaged or married. "How does she know him?"

"Asher is her brother-in-law."

* * *

"Asher is married?" I'm sitting next to Caleb on a small sofa that rests against the back wall of the library. "How is Asher married?"

"He's not," he clarifies with a deep sigh. "He was. It was annulled a few weeks after he got out of rehab."

"Who was he married to?" The question is as foreign as the thought of Asher being married.

"Someone he met in rehab. Her name was Karen. They got married the day he left the facility."

I hadn't wanted to crowd Asher after he'd been released so I had waited until he reached out to me. It was weeks later and by then he was immersed in his work with his brothers. I'd asked about rehab but he had only offered meager facts about the program and therapy.

"Why didn't he say anything?"

He looks directly at me. "I wish I knew the reason. I wish I knew what the hell he was thinking."

"Have you talked to the woman? Karen? Have you spoken to her about Asher?" It's an obvious question but it's one I have to ask.

"I've been trying to locate her all week." He pulls his smartphone from his pocket. "I've been on this thing day and night trying to track her down. I finally found her sister yesterday."

"That's the woman I saw when I came in?" I look at the screen of his phone. "Does she know where Asher is?"

"Her name is Sonia." He shakes his head slightly as he twirls the phone in his palm. "She lives in Vegas. She wouldn't tell me anything unless I flew her and her husband out here."

"What?" I twist towards him on the sofa. "I don't understand."

"She knows how much Asher is worth," he starts before he leans back. "She knows how much we're all worth. She wants money before she'll tell me anything about her sister."

I roll my eyes as I try to piece together what he just told me. "Do you think she actually knows anything about where he is?"

"I think that I'd pay anyone anything at this point just to see my brother again."

TWENTY-SEVEN

"Why did you let her walk out of here?" I ask quietly. "You should have told me who she was when I walked in."

He turns towards me. His eyes are a dark mask covering everything that is lurking beneath the surface of his thoughts and emotions. "You were upset, Rowan. I can't think straight when you're upset."

I close my eyes in a desperate attempt to shield myself from his words. "You can't say things like that to me anymore."

"What?" His hand darts to my bare knee. I'd thought about going home to change into comfortable clothes after work but I had wanted to see Gabriel so much that I'd raced to his apartment still dressed in the white and blue dress I wore to work. Now, sitting next to Caleb with his skin touching mine, I feel completely underdressed yet again.

I don't want to wander off the track that we're on. Finding Asher is the only thing that matters at this point. The fact that I'm still emotionally reeling from what happened in my bed can't factor into anything. I have to push that aside and get my mind back into the game.

"Tell me what's going on." He squeezes my knee and I instinctively pull it away.

"Nothing is going on," I try to say convincingly. "I'm worried about Asher. Did she say anything to you about where he might be before I got here?"

"She didn't." He half-shrugs. "She started talking about money the minute she walked through the door. The woman knows how to negotiate."

"Don't you have people who can track her sister down?" I ask curtly. "You don't need her to give you that information, do you?"

"The private investigator I hired is following up with all of that. Sonia is the direct method. She can give me everything I need."

I nod. I know that it's true. I don't live in a world filled with excess and luxury but I know, based strictly on how Clive conducts his business, that money opens doors that otherwise would be impenetrable. If Caleb can use some of what the brothers have worked so hard for, to help find Asher, it's a no-brainer.

"I want her to tell you where Asher is." I push myself up from the sofa. "I think you should go find her and ask her where he is."

"Before you got here we decided we'd meet tomorrow morning," he chuckles. "I need to go to the bank first."

I shake my head as I turn towards the door. "I have to go. I'm going out of town for work tomorrow. Will you call me once you talk to her again?"

He's on his feet now too. "Where are you going? Why is Clive sending you out of town right now? Doesn't he know that I need you herI don't take any comfort in the words. Instead, a jolting reality takes hold of me. Caleb needs me here. The selfish parts of him want my friendship and comfort to help guide him through the emotions he's feeling because his brother disappeared soon after he had him arrested. "You don't need me here, Caleb. You have Gabriel."

"He doesn't understand me the way you do, Bell."

I loved when he called me that when we were children running up and down the street together trying to launch the kite I got on my birthday from my grandparents. He'd held his hand over mine on the string, pulling me along behind him as we floated the kite just a few feet above the quiet, tree-lined sidewalk. Now, hearing him say it, I'm reminded of that morning when he gave in to his desire for me.

"You're getting closer to finding Asher." I rest my hand on my hip. "I have to do this for work. I need to."

"What's wrong?" His hand reaches out towards me, but he stops it in mid-air. "You've been different since…"

I watch as his fisted hand falls to his side. I lick my bottom lip, wanting my words to portray a strong, unfazed woman. "I've been different since that morning at my apartment. The morning you touched me until I came."

His breath catches and his eyes lock on mine. "Yes. You've changed since then."

This is it. There are defining moments in every relationship. When I was with Tom it was when he told me that he'd rather get high than clean up so he could be a partner to me. With my last boyfriend it was the moment I realized that being away from him was more fulfilling than sitting in a room listening to him talk about himself endlessly. With Caleb, it's right now.

"Do you want me, Caleb? Do you want me in your life other than as a friend?"

The questions pull the air from his lungs. I can tell by the way his body sways forward and his breathing stalls. "What do you mean?"

It's a tactic that he's used since we were children. He'll ask for clarification so he can gather together his tangled thoughts. I've seen him use the approach with his brothers and parents. This is the first time he's ever done it with me.

I close my eyes briefly before I open them and lock eyes with him. "We almost had sex that morning in my apartment. I think we would have if you wouldn't have taken that call. I'm asking you if you want it to happen. Do you want me? Do you want me in that way?"

He crosses his broad arms over his chest as he peers down at me. His lips move slightly before his tongue darts over them. "I think about fucking you all the time."

TWENTY-EIGHT

I didn't see that coming. I thought he'd tell me that we can't be intimate because it would damage our friendship. I actually was counting on him saying that because I had my retort at the ready. In my mind Caleb was going to explain that he valued our friendship so highly that sacrificing it for a few minutes, or in Caleb's case, a few hours of pleasure, would be foolish. I imagined he'd kiss me on my forehead, tell me that I'd find a man who truly deserved me and usher me out of the library, past Ruby and into the night. At the last moment before he shut the door behind me, I'd turn around and tell him that he would never be good enough for me. It would have been a lie but it would have stung him. That entire made up scenario in my mind just went to hell.

Now, I'm staring at his face. I'm staring into the gorgeous face of the man I want to be with and I'm absorbing the fact that he just told me that he thinks about fucking me all the time.

"You think about it too, Bell." His index finger leaps to his lips. "You do, don't you?"

Um, hell yes I do. Morning, noon and night.

"Sometimes," I offer back. "I've thought about it."

"Tell me what you think about." He steps forward a touch, which causes me to instantly retreat a step back. "Tell me what you wanted to do that day."

I can't tell if he's pushing me because he wants me to drop to my knees so I can show him exactly what I wanted to do that day. I'm going to take the bait because a chance like this may never appear again and if I don't tell Caleb Foster exactly what I want, I'll wake up one morning twenty-five years from now next to a man who can't possibly own my pleasure the way Caleb will. "I wanted to feel you inside of me. I wanted to touch you and taste you."

He moves closer still, his expression shifting. "You mean you wanted me to fuck you. You wanted to suck on my cock."

The sheer rawness of his words pulls a blush from deep within me. "Yes. I mean that."

He leans down. He's close. He's so close that I can feel the feathery soft touch of his breath on my lips each time he exhales. "You wanted me to lick your pussy, didn't you, Rowan?"

I've never heard the word from any man I've been with before. It's always felt too intimate but now it pulls something from deep within me. My sex aches. "Yes."

"You wanted me to eat you until you screamed my name." He pushes a piece of my hair off my forehead. "Then you wanted me to flip you over so I could fuck you hard."

I know I should pull back so I can breathe but I'm frozen in place. "Caleb."

"I thought about it this morning." He brushes his soft lips against my cheek. "I stroked my cock thinking about sliding inside your tight, little pussy."

I'm so aroused I feel as though I could come just from listening to him talk. I don't say anything. I only lean forward hoping to feel the touch of his lips against mine.

"If I fuck you once, I won't be able to stop. I'll want it more. I'll never be able to give it up."

I look up into his dark eyes. "You don't need to stop."

The pad of his thumb traces a path over my bottom lip. "I will destroy you, Rowan."

"You can't destroy me." I dart my tongue out to catch the tip of his thumb.

He looks down at my mouth, his own tongue licking his bottom lip. "I don't know how to love a woman. I will use you. I will hurt you. I will damage you in ways you don't understand."

"No." I shake my head slightly from side-to-side. "You're wrong."

"I'm right. I know myself. I'll hurt you. I'll ruin you."

"I'll risk it." I whisper before I close my eyes and press my mouth into his.

He groans into our kiss, his hands cupping my face. He tilts my head slightly so he can control the pressure of our lips against each other. A low moan escapes his body and floats into mine as his breath quickens.

I feel his erection pressed against me, straining against the fabric of his pants. My hand drops to his belt. I fumble briefly with it before I undo the clasp. Just as my fingers drop to his zipper, he pulls back from our kiss.

"Bell, Christ, please don't." His voice aches with the same desire I feel inside of me. "I can't want you like this. I can't do it."

I'm not one to throw myself at a man but when it's the one man I've always longed to be with, I'm willing to toss tradition out the window. "Let me taste you, Caleb. I want you to come in my mouth."

"Fuck." His lips brush over mine again. "I'm going to explode."

I push both my hands towards the front of his pants. I stroke his long, hard cock through the fabric. "I want this so much."

His hands leap to my face again. "One taste of you will ruin us both. I can't let myself hurt you."

"Caleb,'" I say his name softly as I pull back to look into his eyes. I want him. I've never wanted anything in my life more than I want him but I won't beg. His resistance is real. I not only hear it, but I feel it in his kiss and touch. "Tell me to go if you don't want me."

"It's not that simple." His hands press into my cheeks. "I want you so much. I crave you, Bell."

I try to break free of his touch but he holds steady, keeping his eyes locked on mine.

"I want to push you against that wall and fuck you." He nods his chin towards the wall behind us. "I want to feel you around me. I want to be inside of you."

"Do it," I challenge. "Fuck me, Caleb."

"Shit." His hands fall from my face. "Don't say that. I can't hear that."

It shouldn't be this complicated. The man says he wants me. His body is screaming it and yet he keeps pulling back. "Tell me what you want."

"I want you," he says the words so quickly they meld together. "I want you."

"I'm right here." I smooth my hands over my chest. "You can have me right now."

The tortured look on his face speaks volumes to me before he even opens his mouth. He's fighting a battle within himself. It's a battle born from his desire for my body versus his need for my friendship. "I need you so much. You mean everything to me. I try to control it but sometimes I can't. Today…now…I just couldn't stop but I have to."

I feel the tears barreling through me before they hit my eyes. I wipe my face hoping that will quiet the pain that I feel over the stark realization that regardless of how much he wants me, he'll never take me. "You don't want to make love to me, do you, Caleb?"

I cringe at the shaky sound of my own voice as I say the words. They sound pitiful and hopeless. They're the words of a woman who wants a man so much that she's willing to trade every ounce of her self-worth just to crawl into bed with him. That's not who I am. It's never been who I am.

He bites his bottom lip as he rubs his hand over the back of his neck. "You are the only woman I want to make love to. You're also the only friend I have. I can't risk losing that. I can't."

I can't find words to say in response. I just stare at him wishing I had followed my better judgement and gone home after seeing Gabriel.

"I destroy the people I love." He inhales sharply. "I caused my parent's divorce, I almost ruined Asher's life, I've damaged my relationship with Gabriel and I broke Vena completely. I can't do that to you."

Hearing him say Vena's name jars something within me. It pulls me back to the time when they got engaged and the hope that was there in his eyes. I haven't seen that again. It's gone just as that uncontrollable feeling of desire for him that owned my body not more than five minutes is gone. "I need to go. I need some space. Time, maybe…I can't be your friend right now."

He doesn't respond. There's no effort to stop me as I pick up my purse and walk away.

TWENTY-NINE

"If Libby didn't need me here, I'd be on that plane with you." Graham rummages through my dresser drawer. "I like this one. You should take it."

I turn to see him holding a very small white bikini top in his hand. "I haven't worn that in years. I doubt that I'd fit into it now."

"It's perfect then." He smiles broadly as he fishes the matching bottoms from the depths of the drawer. "There are all kinds of single men in the Hamptons at this time of year. You can dazzle them with your body in this."

"I'll more likely be flashing them my body if I wear that." I nod towards the drawer. "There's a black one piece in there that I'll take."

"Like hell you will," he snaps back. "It's bikinis only. I've seen you naked, Rowan. Damn, you're fine."

I arch a brow as I turn my head to look directly at him. "You've never seen me naked."

"I have," he counters. "You were walking around the apartment in the buff one day when you thought I was out. I saw it all."

I blush from the knowledge that he saw me completely nude. "That makes everything awkward."

He throws back his head in laughter. "It does not. Your body does nothing for me. Nothing."

I reach forward to kiss his forehead. "I really needed this. I'm glad you came home early."

"Me too." He folds a white cardigan before placing it in the small suitcase that's opened on my bed. "After being clit teased like that, you need to blow off some steam."

I smile softly. "Clit teased? Is that what we're going to call it?"

"I call it like I see it." He holds up a peach colored blouse. "Do you want to take this?"

I shudder at the sight of that. "Throw that one in the donation pile. My mother sent me that last year as a birthday gift. I told her once, when I was seven-years-old, that peach was my favorite color. She's never forgotten."

"Moms make it their job to remember things like that." He tosses the shirt onto a small pile of clothes on the floor. "When is she coming to visit? I can't wait to meet her."

"She usually comes around the holidays." I hold up a navy blazer. "Do you think I need to take this?"

"I think you can get away with a skirt and blouse for the meeting or," he begins before he marches across the room to my walk-in closet. "I'd wear this to the meeting if I was you, or if I was a woman."

I glance up at the light blue dress he's holding in his hand. "I like that one. How did you know I had that? I don't think I've worn it since you've moved in."

"I pick up your dry cleaning sometimes." He pulls the dress from the hanger before rolling it neatly and placing it in the suitcase. "I checked out your wardrobe."

"I like that," I whisper. I do like it. I like having someone close who wants to take care of me. It's not that I'm not completely capable of taking care of myself. I am, but the knowledge that someone is there, to pick up my dry cleaning or help me pack, means a lot to me.

"We can talk about Caleb." He doesn't look up from the suitcase. He's busying his hands with moving the articles of clothing around to make more room. "I know it stings."

What happened in Caleb's apartment doesn't just sting. It bites through to my core. I'd taken the subway back to my place after I'd left his building. I'd texted Ivy first wanting to melt into the arms of my best friend. I needed an outlet and listening to her talk about her family and what's going on in her shop, would have stolen my thoughts away from Caleb. It may have only been a temporary escape, but that's all I need.

She hadn't responded so I'd called Graham who was out for dinner with a friend of Libby's. I'd insisted he not hurry home but when he heard the brittle emotion in my voice, he promised he'd be waiting in our apartment, with chocolate and a shoulder to lean on.

"He wanted me." I feel a blush race over my face when I say the words. "I'm not being egotistical, Graham. I mean he said he wanted to fuck me."

His chin dips up so our eyes meet. "You told him that you wanted him too?"

"I did," I mutter wishing with everything that I am, that I hadn't. "I thought it was my chance to be brutally honest so I put it all out there."

"Put it all out there?" He straightens, resting his hand on his hip. "What exactly did you say to him?"

When I said those intimate words to Caleb it came from a place of desperate want. I'd never once blatantly told a man I wanted to suck his cock. I've never used the word 'fuck' with a man either. I haven't hidden my longing for the men I've been with, but it's always been shielded behind a veil of timidity. The thought of letting all of my inhibitions loose was tempered in the past by the knowledge that I'd have to face the man the next day. With Caleb it's different. I wasn't ashamed of my primal desire for him. I owned it and look what it got me.

"Rowan?" Graham rifles through my drawer pulling out a pair of silver earrings. "I'll put these in the side pocket. You'll remember they're there, right?"

I nod sheepishly. "I told him I wanted to suck him off and that I wanted him to…you know…I just went for it and told him I wanted him to fuck me."

Both of his brows pop up as he leans back against the dresser, crossing his legs at the ankle. "You're telling me that you threw yourself at him, while you were wearing that killer dress and the man turned you down?"

"You're making me sound pathetic," I say half-jokingly. "He wanted me. I could tell that he did but he kept talking about our friendship and hurting me."

"You think it was just an excuse? Do you honestly think he made that up to avoid having sex with you?"

It's so straightforward and simple that I have to stop and think about my answer. "I think he believes that he'll hurt me if we cross the line from friends to lovers. Caleb needs me as a friend."

He scratches the top of his head, which causes his hair to fall down into his eyes. He brushes it away with a swipe of his hand. "If a guy tells you straight up that he's bad news, you have to believe him. Stay away from him, Rowan. If he says he'll hurt you, he means it."

THIRTY

I rest my head on the uncomfortable airport lounge chair as I reread the text message conversation I just had with Gabriel. After Graham had helped me pack, he'd given me a sweet kiss on the cheek and literally tucked me into bed last night. I woke at six to find a note on the kitchen table from him. He'd prepared a fruit salad for me to take with me and there was a car service waiting outside the building to whisk me to the airport. If I didn't consider Graham a close friend before last night, all of that has shifted.

I'd texted Gabriel in the car to tell him that I was taking him up on the offer to stay at the Foster house in the Hamptons for the weekend. I was mildly surprised when he texted me back immediately. My own sleep has been sporadic since Asher's been missing so I'm not shocked that Gabriel was wide awake just after six. He promised me he'd let me know the minute he hears from Asher and I made the same promise in return.

I open my email and scroll down the list of new messages. The majority are work related and given the short duration of the flight, I know that I won't have time to answer any of them when I'm in the air. I forward a trio of the urgent ones to Clive, along with a text asking him to reply to them as soon as he gets them.

I scroll back to my text messages and swipe my thumb down to Asher's name. I type out a short message telling him I miss him and I'll be away for a few days but he can call at any time. I stare at the screen willing the new message icon to pop up but there's nothing. Asher still isn't responding and even though I'm clinging tightly to the notion that he's fine and has tucked himself away so he can deal with whatever has pulled him down, I know that sooner or later I'm going to have to face the reality that he may not come back, or he may be unable to. It's too soon to think that yet though and for this weekend at least, I'm going to believe he's healthy, safe and thinking about coming home.

I draw in a heavy breath as I hear the announcement of my flight. My heart may not want to leave New York, even if it's just for a few days, but my mind needs to. With any luck, I'll find the serenity I need to come back here, stronger, more focused and less Caleb Foster obsessed.

* * *

"You'll stay for lunch, dear." His brows pop up in excited anticipation. "We're having fish today. You like fish, don't you?"

It's not my first choice but I'm not one to be picky when the invitation is coming from one of the sweetest people I've ever met.

When Clive told me I needed to fly out to Martha's Vineyard to secure the transfer of the rights to a software program, I had visions of meeting an arrogant developer who would fight me tooth and nail on every detail. Instead, I was greeted at the door of a quaint cottage by a man in his eighties who has an office filled with computers, a garden overflowing with roses and a smile that could melt the heart of even the darkest soul.

Ernie Jacobs has a brilliant mind and a lonely heart. I sensed it the moment he led me into this sitting room. The furniture consists of a perfect blend of modern pieces and antiques and the walls are dotted with photographs of a beautiful woman. They create a timeline of a rich life. I studied the image of the blonde haired beauty standing next to a young Ernie as they pledged their vows on their wedding day. The holiday family portrait of the two of them surrounded by their children and grandchildren captures the spirit of joy that is present in all their faces and the image of an elderly woman in the garden staring at the man behind the camera with a look of tender adoration in her eyes, speaks of a love that knows no boundaries of time or circumstance.

"She passed just last year." His voice cracks. "It's hard not to stare, isn't it? She was the most beautiful thing in the world."

I don't know much about enduring love. My parents' marriage fell apart beneath the burden of my father's affair. My mother couldn't shoulder the pain and she'd thrown him out into the street, literally. He'd come home from work one day to find everything he owned, scattered in a thoughtless mess on the sidewalk in front of our townhouse. It had been the beginning of the end of our ideal family. It all came to a crashing halt in the corridor of a courtroom in

Queens with vile words being thrown around. I'd managed to maintain a relationship with each of my parents but with my mother in Florida and my father in Connecticut, it meant once-a-year visits and empty conversations on the phon"She was very lovely," I concur. "I'd really like to stay for lunch."

"That's fantastic." He claps his hands together. "It will give me time to show you the other programs I've developed."

"There's more?" I ask with a wide grin on my face. This man knows more about computer software than almost anyone I've ever met which says a lot considering the fact that I work for the most influential tech company on the east coast.

"I've put together some apps." He winks at me. "Some of them are for young folks like you."

"You know what an app is?" I try not to giggle as I ask.

He taps the bottom of his cane against the arm of the chair I'm sitting in. "Mark my words, you're going to want the rights to every single app I have."

THIRTY-ONE

"Carly will drive you down to the ferry, dear." He limps across the floor towards my suitcase and purse. "Are you meeting your fellow in the Hamptons?"

It's a question that I should have seen coming. Ernie may have a pulse on what's hot in the tech world but when it comes to romance the man is old school through and through. The stories he told over our three course lunch about the endearing things he did for his late wife are proof of that. He's a keeper and if I was an octogenarian, I'd be making a fast move on this man.

"I don't have a fellow at the moment," I say with a small smile. It's been longer than a moment if I'm being honest.

He pushes the wire rimmed glasses he's wearing to the tip of his nose so he can peer over them. "You don't have a fellow? How is that possible?"

Flattery is the only thing I need right now after Caleb turned me down on the spot last night. I should ask Ernie if can stay the weekend in his guest room. The man is full of compliments, which means my self-esteem meter would be off the charts by Sunday evening. "Men in New York are fickle. I'm still looking for the right one."

"The right one will almost always be a friend first. If you have a fellow who is a friend and you have a sweet spot for him, he might be the one."

Or he might be a raving lunatic who thinks it's entertaining to talk dirty to me before he rejects me. "I don't have any friends who would be the right one."

"Don't be too quick to rule out a friend." He gently grabs my elbow as he leads us out of the dining room. "You never know when love is waiting around the corner."

I used to think that. Now I know better. When it comes to Caleb the only thing waiting for me is a fractured friendship and the embarrassment of knowing I poured out all of my deepest desires to him and he shut me down.

* * *

"You want to go back to Martha's Vineyard?" Clive's voice breaks up slightly as he asks the question.

I turn up the volume on my phone, hoping that it will drown out all of the traffic noise. Clive had thoughtfully arranged to have me picked up at the ferry dock by a private driver. He'd made certain that the car was a convertible, which would have been spectacular given the gorgeous weather and scenic views. The problem is that I can barely hear anything he's saying to me so I can only assume the same is true on his end. "Ernie has developed a lot of great stuff. He's willing to sell the rights to us if we want them. I think we have to jump on it."

"What?" He yells into the receiver. "I can't hear you, Rowan."

I laugh out loud, letting the warm air race over my face as I throw my head back. I haven't been out of New York City in months and today, I'm realizing just how much I needed the break. I hold the phone close to my lips as I scream into it. "I'll call you back as soon as I'm at the house."

I end the call before I toss the phone back into my purse. I tap the driver on the shoulder. "Is there a store near the house? I want to pick up a few supplies for the weekend."

He nods without taking his eyes off the road.

I lean back into the seat and close my eyes. This weekend is my chance to decompress and unwind. I'm going to push work aside, focus on the new books I downloaded to my e-reader and let every thought I have of Caleb Foster and his brothers disappear from my mind.

* * *

I climb into the backseat of the car again noting that the horizon looks serene now that dusk is starting to fall. I'd taken a few minutes to go into a local store to buy the essentials. I purchased coffee, fresh pressed juice, some fruit, wine, cheese and bread. It's everything that I've been craving and everything that my body needs. I have no intention of leaving the house once the driver takes me there.

"The reception is great here." The driver's voice startles me. "I heard you having trouble with a call earlier. You can make it now. I can go grab a coffee."

I glance down at my phone and realize that Clive may be leaving the office soon. Our conversation would go a lot smoother if he had access to his computer. I can send him the notes on the apps that Ernie emailed to me.

"That would actually be great," I say with a flourish of my hand. "I'll need thirty minutes or so. Does that work for you or do you need to be somewhere?"

"I'm at your disposal all weekend, Ms. Bell." A thin smile covers his mouth. "Mr. Parker said I should be available in case you need me."

"Once you drop me at the house, I don't need you until Sunday at four." I scroll my index finger over my phone's screen. "I'll call Clive and then we'll head out, okay?"

He hands me a plain white card with a ten digit phone number on it. "Call me when you're ready to go, and I'll be back."

I nod as I press the screen to dial Clive's office. This is my last official duty before I cut myself off from civilization for the weekend.

THIRTY-TWO

I watch Seth, the driver Clive hired, as he backs the car out of the driveway. He'd insisted on helping me bring my suitcase and bags to the door. He wanted to go inside the house with me to check to make certain everything was in working order, but I'd patiently declined. I haven't been to the Foster house in almost a decade. It looks exactly as I remember it. The green shutters are still a fitting and elegant contrast to the white siding that covers the outside of the house. The trees in the front yard are larger and the stone walkway that leads to the front door is now chipped and overgrown with grass. The essence of the place is exactly as it was when we filled the rooms with laughter during the summer. We'd race down to the beach and while the boys swam in the water, I'd collect rocks and shells on the sand.

CHANCE

I fish for the keys Gabriel gave to me in my purse. I sigh as I feel my fingers grab hold of them. I examine them under the light that is streaming from the lantern hung above the porch. I twist the key in the lock and shiver as I feel it give way. I swing open the door with one hand while I grab the handle of my suitcase with the other.

I run my hand along the wall near the door hopeful that I'll connect with a light switch. I do. The room fills with muted light and I soak in the surroundings.

The main room is elegant and although some of the furniture is covered with white sheets, I feel at home immediately. I'd sat on the green and blue checkered sofa when I played chess with Gabriel and I'd learned how to play a simple tune on the piano in the corner when Asher had a spare moment one rainy afternoon. This place speaks of my childhood and my connection to the Foster family and I realize that in my haste to get away from Caleb I've taken myself back to the heart of our connection.

I walk across the room to stare out into the blackness that envelops the back yard. The beach is just beyond it but I can't see it now. All I can see in my mind's eye is the last day

I was in the house when I was fifteen. Miles had gone for a ride with Gabriel and Asher was embroiled in a heated tennis tournament that took him away from all of us for most of the week we were there.

I'd stood in this very spot, overlooking the yard while watching Caleb. He had just come back from the beach. His hair was a wet mess and it clung to the side of his handsome face. He was as tall then as he is now and back when I was a teenager he was imposing, dark and mysterious.

I remember every vivid detail of the day and just as I was about to walk away from the windows, he pulled a towel from a pile that his mother kept near the door for the boys to wipe their feet before they came into the house.

His eyes had darted around the yard but they never settled on the house and with baited breath I stood frozen watching as he turned to the side and slowly pushed his damp swim trunks from his body. It was the first time I'd seen a man naked. I knew that I should look away but I was mesmerized by the sculpted tone of his stomach and the gentle curve of his ass.

I caught a brief glimpse of his cock when he turned towards the house, before he wrapped the towel around him. By the time he walked through the patio doors and into the room, I was nestled on the couch, a book open on my lap.

He grunted something to me as he walked by and I looked up, staring at the strong muscles of his back and calves as he walked down the hallway towards his bedroom. I never told him about what I saw. I never told anyone. It was my secret and I've carried it with me through every relationship I've ever had.

I close my eyes as I lean my head against the cool glass and try to gaze out into the yard. I'll see the spot where he was standing tomorrow morning once the sun rises. For tonight, I'll lay in silence in the same bed I laid in that night after I saw his beautiful body and I'll dream the same dreams about my desire for him. The difference is now that I've felt the kind of pleasure he can give to a woman and that is a bittersweet torture in itself.

I feel my emotions rising to the surface. I knew that I'd feel something coming back here but I never imagined that the teenage crush I had on Caleb could feel so real so many years later. I need to forget about him. I need to say goodbye to what I've wanted with him and this feels like the perfect place to do that. I'm alone. I'm strong and I'm ready to move forward without my Caleb Foster fantasies in tow.

I gaze out into the darkness one last time and that's when I feel it.

I don't scream.

I don't panic.

I just reach up to grab the hand that's now resting on my shoulder.

I didn't hear him come in. He may have been here all along but I know it's him.

I turn slowly, look up and whisper his name.

THIRTY-THREE

"I knew it would be you who found me." Asher traces the pad of his thumb over my eyebrow. "I kept telling myself that you'd remember how much I loved this place."

I nod slowly. I haven't been able to say anything other than his name since I turned around. He's sporting a full beard, his hair is longer than it was the last time I saw him and he's happy. He's happier than I've seen him in years.

"I'm sorry I haven't returned any of your text messages or calls." He reaches to hold my hand in his. "I had to get away. I was scared, Bell. I was worried that I'd start using again if I stayed."

"Asher," I repeat his name. "I've been so worried. Everyone is worried."

"I know." He rakes his hand through his hair, pushing it back from his face. "I thought

I'd come up for a day or two but then it was a week, and then longer and I didn't know how to come back."

"The police are looking for you." I step towards the checkered sofa. "I need to sit down."

He scoops his hand around my waist, leading me towards the furniture. "They were here. They came to the door but I didn't answer. They just left. That was days ago."

I can't say that I'm shocked that there was no follow up. Asher is a grown man. The police must receive dozens of missing person's reports a day. I'm certain that the majority of the resources are focused on children who are either abducted by a parent or stranger.

"You said you were going to visit your mom." I sit as I try to level my breathing. "You never went there."

"I wanted to be alone." He leans back and skims his hand over the leg of his jeans. "I needed time to process some stuff. My mom wouldn't have helped with that."

It's a weak excuse. There's no way he wasn't aware of the turmoil and pain that he was causing everyone who cared about him, me included. "You just disappeared. I don't understand how you could do that."

I see the pain in his face as soon as the words leave my mouth. I've been mindful of what I say to him since he came back from rehab. I haven't wanted to push him and now I'm realizing that it's given him a cushion that's allowed him to be selfish.

"I'm sorry." His voice cracks slightly. "I was planning on calling Gabriel this weekend."

I want to believe him but given the fact that I accidentally stumbled on his hiding place, I can't do it. "Why didn't you call him last week or the week before that? You know how much he worries about you."

"I couldn't do it." He leans back into the soft cushions of the sofa. "I have to explain why I took off. Gabriel is going to want to know."

Newsflash, Asher. Everyone wants to know.

"Why did you leave?" I ask hoping that he'll give me an explanation.

He shakes his head lightly from side-to-side. "I don't do this grown up thing very well. I suck at being a responsible adult."

I feel a small smile tug at the corner of my lips. "I'm not going to argue with you about that."

"I'll call him now." He stretches his legs out to reach inside the front pocket of his jeans to retrieve his phone. "I need to charge it. It ran out of juice a few days ago. I stopped charging it because…"

He stopped charging it because when you're trying to escape from the realities of life, a phone isn't your ally.

"You can use my phone to call him." I reach towards the coffee table to grab my purse. I pull my smartphone out quickly. It doesn't take me more than a few seconds to bring up Gabriel's contact information. "Call him now. Tell him you're okay."

He scoops my phone into his palm, presses the phone icon and brings it to his ear.

* * *

"You're sure you don't want to come back to Manhattan with me?" Asher pushes a sweatshirt into a large duffel bag. "It would help if you'd come see Gabriel with me."

The only person I would be helping is Asher. I planned on coming to the house for some rest and relaxation. I may have solved the great mystery of where Asher has been hiding but that's where my part in this twisted Foster saga ends. Responsibility is a bitter pill to swallow for some people and I'd definitely put Asher into that category. "I'm staying here. You need to handle it by yourself."

He tilts his chin up in a slight act of defiance. "Did you come looking for me, Bell? Did you know I'd be here?"

I could tell a small white lie that would give him some reassurance about the unspoken strength of our friendship, but false hope isn't what he needs right now. "No, Asher. I was taking care of some business on Martha's Vineyard yesterday and Gabriel suggested I come here to get away from things."

There's no masking the disappointment in his expression. "You didn't seem surprised to see me last night. It felt like you knew I'd be here waiting for you."

I look down at the hardwood floor. There's a stain on one of the boards. I remember exactly how it got there. Asher and I had found a stray puppy down by the beach and in our infinite, and grade school, wisdom we had smuggled it into his room. It hadn't gone through the rigors of being housebroken so it had relieved itself wherever it saw fit. The stain I'm looking at now is a reminder of that time when we were young, innocent and unaware of real consequences.

"I've been looking for you around every corner for weeks." I lean my leg against the bed. "Every time my phone rang, I hoped it was you. I came here to escape that. I was so tired of worrying."

"I've let you down." He sweeps his hand across his brow. "I've let everyone down again."

"You're going back now." I point to his bag. "You should finish packing. The car Gabriel sent for you will be here soon."

"Will you call me when you're back in the city? You'll call me, right?"

"You need time to sort out things with your brothers." I start towards the bedroom door. "Once things have settled, call me and we'll talk."

THIRTY-FOUR

There's something wickedly decadent about shutting yourself off from the world. I've only been alone in the house for a few hours and I can sense the pull that Asher felt. Once he left, I'd called Clive to tell him that I wouldn't be back to the office until Wednesday. I shot off a short text message to Graham after that telling him to expect me back at home mid-week and then I'd turned off my phone and tablet and buried them in a drawer in the guest room. I have my pick of rooms since the house is completely vacant but the familiarity of that room called to me. I had unpacked the few items I brought with me last night and had fallen asleep in that bed.

I break off a large chunk of bread before slicing some cheese and placing it all on a small, square plate. I pour myself a half a glass of the deep bodied red wine I bought yesterday. It's lunch for me and as soon as I'm done indulging my hunger, my plan is to head down to the beach to lie in the sun.

I take my snack outside to the large table that has always inhabited the west corner of the yard. We'd gather around this spot when we were children to wait for the dinners that the cook prepared for us. Miles and I were always hesitant to try new things, given the fact that our mother never ventured far off the baked chicken path. It was here, in this spot, that I found my love for fresh shucked oysters and charcoal grilled corn on the cob.

I sit in silence as I eat, pulling the clean air into my lungs. Sipping the wine slowly, not wanting to slip into the edges of feeling lightheaded or sleepy. I want to embrace the day and enjoy it.

"Rowan Bell?" A man's voice carries through the silence. "That's not you, is it?"

It's me but right now I wish it wasn't. I can feel eyes peering over the fence at me. I know who lives next door. It's Ian Handler. He was Caleb's best friend for years. He lived in the city too and each summer he'd catch a ride with the Fosters out to his family home here. I look to the left knowing that it's a move I'm going to inevitably regret. Apparently the universe is determined to spare me the luxury of having any time to myself this weekend.

"It is you." He smiles at me and his top teeth instantly pop into view. I remember vividly the way his two front teeth subtly overlap each other. There was one summer, when I must have been either thirteen or fourteen-years-old when I found his smile alluring. To be honest, I found everything about him appealing for a brief span of time. I see why when I look at him now. His face is still ruggedly handsome and his hair is now shorter, but still the same rich black that it was back then.

"Ian." I know I should stand but I don't. That would be a silent invitation for him to engage me in a conversation I don't want to have. "How are you?"

"I'm great." He pops out of view and I cringe. I know what it means. He's on his way to the gate that separates the two yards.

I finish the last mouthful of wine in my glass before I lick my lips, sweeping up any wayward droplets. I slide the linen napkin I found in the kitchen over my mouth and I ready myself for the bear hug I know is just seconds away.

"Rowan." As if on cue, he's standing no more than three feet away from me. "Come here and give me a hug."

I stand slowly, biding my time until I embrace him. I scratch the back of my neck before I pull on the hem of the short sundress I have on.

His arms are around me in an instant. I'm consumed with the scent of his skin. It's cologne inspired by the outdoors. He smells like a walk in the forest. It's strangely pleasant.

"You look exactly like I remember you." His voice is deep and gruff.

"You do too, Ian."

"Are you here with Asher?" He looks over my shoulder to the empty plate and wineglass sitting atop the dining table. "When I saw him yesterday he didn't say anything about you coming up."

It's an out that I know I shouldn't take but given the fact that I can feel the beginnings of an erection through the thin swim trunks he's wearing, I'm going to use his assumptions to my own advantage. "I surprised him. I arrived last nigh"I bet he's happy to see you." He leans back and my eyes involuntarily fall to the overwhelming bulge that seems to keep growing and growing. I pull my gaze back up quickly but not before he notices. "You're almost as hot as I remember you."

Thank you, I think?

"Speaking of hot," I begin before I let out a raucous fake laugh.

He doesn't even crack a smile.

""Speaking of hot," I repeat with a lot less enthusiasm this time. "I'm heading back inside. I'm not used to the sun."

"I'll come by later with some beers." He squeezes my arms. "It's so good to see you, Rowan."

"Good to see you too," I mumble under my breath as I make a beeline for the patio doors and the quiet serenity of the empty house.

THIRTY-FIVE

I smooth some of the scented lotion that Graham tossed into my suitcase over my legs. I'd soaked my body in a hot bath for more than an hour. The water may have been chilled by the time I got out, but the stress it pulled from me made it worth the discomfort.

I wrap the thin robe I found in the closet in my room around my body. The temperature dips when night falls in this part of the state, but even though I'm tempted to turn up the thermostat to blast some warm air into the space, I know that I'll sleep more soundly if I don't. I may even crack open a window in my bedroom so I can drift off listening to the silence that is never present in Manhattan.

I'd heard a loud knock on the front door when I was drawing my bath. At any other time, I may have invited Ian in to share a beer and if I wasn't so intent on focusing on myself this weekend, I may even have been tempted to jump into bed with him. It would have been nothing but a quick escape from my life and a way to feel the pleasure I've been longing for.

I doubt that I'll ever come back to this place after I leave it in a few days and that assurance makes the possibility of a rendezvous with Ian that much more appealing.

It's not who I am though. I've never had a one night stand and I don't see myself pursuing it now. I want more than that. I need it and once I'm back in New York I may actually reach out to that chef that Ivy wants to set me up with.

I glance at the clock on the bedside table and realize that it's barely past ten. My imagination had envisioned me sitting out on the patio at midnight with a glass of wine under the stars. My reality is that I'm too tired to even venture out of the room to turn off the lights in the hallway. I do the only thing I can. I slip the robe off my body, slide between the cool sheets and close my eyes.

* * *

I feel the warmth of the sun on the side of my face and I realize that it's morning already. It's been so long since I've slept through the night that I sigh loudly. I don't open my eyes as I kick the blanket and thin sheet off my body. I stretch out, indulging in the freedom of not having any restrictions at all.

I drank too much wine and too little water yesterday. My mouth is dry and I feel the beginnings of a headache coming on. I swing my long legs over the side of the bed and shiver when I feel the cool air wafting through the open window hit my back.

I reach blindly for the robe, knowing that I dropped it on the bed before I fell asleep. I find it and the moment I've pulled it around me, I feel better.

I take the wooden stairs slowly and cautiously. I'm still sleepy and in the middle of an unfamiliar house. I left my purse, with a vial of ibuprofen in it, in the living room.

Once I down two pills with a half a bottle of chilled water, I brush my teeth wanting to rid my mouth of the dry feeling I woke up with. I glance at the clock that is hanging on the wall in the hallway. It's barely past six.

I walk back into my bedroom, tossing the robe onto the bed as I move past it. I stop at the window. I pull open the curtains just enough to see the view. It's not ideal but I can spot the ocean through the tops of the trees. It's nothing like the view from my apartment in Manhattan. This is everything that life in the city can't offer to me.

I inch backwards until I feel the bed behind me. I fall back onto the pillow and sleep consumes me almost instantly. I'm just falling into the throes of a dream when I hear a soft tap in the room. I don't open my eyes. It's the bottom of the blind that normally covers the window at night. I hadn't closed it because I wanted to wake to the sun.

I turn onto my back, allowing my mind to go blank, wanting sleep to grab hold of me for at least a few more hours but I hear the noise again. It's louder this time.

I tilt my chin up, pushing my head back into the pillow. I should have paid more attention during yoga class when the yogi spoke of shutting off the world and finding your center.

I feel a brush against my arm and this time my eyes fly open.

My heart races.

My breathing stops.

He's standing next to the bed.

His hair is a tousled mess. His jaw covered with stubble.

He looks dangerous, desirous and as his eyes rake over my body, I know that my life will never be the same again.

THIRTY-SIX

I watch in silence as he pushes the dress shirt he's wearing from his shoulders. His hands work quickly on his belt and I can't take my eyes off of his body when he kicks free of his pants. I stare at his cock without any shame. It's beautiful. It's thick, long and hard.

He doesn't say anything as he slides into the bed next to me, pulling me into his chest. I wrap my arms around his torso and bury my face in his neck.

His arms are around me; his hands cupping my bare ass. He sighs as I curve my body into his. I want him to touch me. I want him to kiss me. I want to feel him inside of me but most of all I want to breathe in the scent of his skin and listen to the beat of his heart.

"I can't stay away from you, Bell," he says hoarsely. "I can't do it."

I push my body into his, wanting to lessen the small amount of physical distance that still exists between us. "I don't want you to stay away, Caleb."

"I'll hurt you." His voice cracks slightly. "It will kill me to hurt you."

"It won't happen." I turn my head so I can press my lips against the smooth skin of his muscular chest. "It's not going to happen."

His hand flies to the back of my head, pulling at my hair so hard that I have no choice but to tilt my neck to look up at him as he speaks. "You're my only weakness. It's always been you."

His lips seal over mine in a deep and lush kiss. His breath tastes like coffee and peppermint and his tongue glides over my bottom lip with the promise of pleasure I've never known before. He growls my name into my mouth before he pulls back.

"I couldn't stay away." He weaves his hand through my hair. "I knew you were here. I couldn't function. I had to come."

I nod slowly as I stare into his eyes. "I wanted you to come. I've been waiting forever for you."

He rolls me back onto my back in one quick movement and then he's hovering above me. I soak in the strong details of his face. I study the chiseled features of the man I've yearned for since I knew what intimacy was.

"I wanted to be your first," he says softly as he blinks slowly. "I always wanted to be your first, Bell."

Everything I feel catches in my throat and I can barely talk. "I wanted that too."

"I came to your graduation to tell you how I felt." His lips feather across my cheek. "I went to college and thought about you every day."

I reach up to graze my hand across the back of his neck. It pulls a shiver from him. I know my heart. I know that if we share ourselves with each other and he pulls away, that I'll be left in a deep pit of self-loathing and depression. He's warned me. He's told me he's going to hurt me and I know the risks. I also know that I need him. I pull gently on his neck, guiding his mouth to mine before I sink my teeth into his bottom lip and feel the brush of his cock against my hip.

He kisses me deeply, his tongue gliding against mine in an achingly slow dance. I crave the taste of his mouth so I cling to him tightly as he kisses me harder. His hand falls to my breast, his fingers pinching my swollen nipple, pulling a deep and guttural groan from my core.

I whimper when he pulls back slightly. He stares into my face, his expression stoic and strong. For a half beat of my heart I panic, wondering if he's thinking the same thoughts that overtook him that day in his apartment. I breathe again when his eyes follow the path of his hand and he looks down at my body.

My hips move involuntarily as soon as he starts to lower himself to my core. I close my eyes, uncertain about whether I can stand a single lash of his soft tongue against my tender flesh. I'm aroused. I'm so aroused just from his kiss.

He rests his head on my thigh as he runs his index finger over my smooth cleft. "Your pussy is so beautiful. It's perfect."

I blush at the words. Not just because of the frank rawness of them, but also because of the tender way he says them. My hands fall to his head, wanting to guide him.

He's spurred on by my actions and licks the length of my folds in one slow movement. I arch my ass off the bed wanting to feel more.

He dives in, his tongue expertly focused on my clit, his hands cupped beneath me, pulling me into him.

I moan loudly into the still air. I don't want to quiet anything I'm feeling. I don't want to mask what I want. I'm going to take everything I can from him because I know it's what he's going to do to me. He'll give and then he'll expect to receive. I want it, he does too.

His tongue flickers over my clit, drawing my heated desire to the surface before he slows the pace, pulling me back from the edge. It's a torturous ride and just when I'm sure that I'm about to fall into the clutches of an intense orgasm, he pulls back, rubbing his finger over my core, telling me to wait.

"I want to come," I say quietly. "I'm aching."

"You're so wet." He laps at me loudly. "I could keep you on edge for hours just so I can taste this."

I cry out both in pleasure and agony. "Lick it. Just suck it and make me come."

"My cock is so hard." I feel his hand drop and I know he's stroking the thick root. "I can't wait to feel myself inside of you."

His words only add to my need to find release. I drop my hand from his head, wanting to bring myself to the edge.

"No," he says gruffly. "It's not for you to take."

I kick my leg softly, frustrated by his need to tease me endlessly. "Fuck me then. Just fuck me."

He looks up, his gaze catching mine. "You're going to come on my lips. I'm going to taste it all."

With that he lowers his mouth to my core. He pulls my ass of the bed, levels his tongue against my clit and licks me hard, fast and furiously until I come screaming his name.

THIRTY-SEVEN

I run my hand over his sheathed cock. I'd ripped the condom package from his hands, wanting to touch him before he was ready for that to happen. I'd carefully placed the condom over him, rolling it down, running my hands over his thick root.

I kiss his thigh wishing I had taken him in my mouth before I covered him. I want to taste him. I want to feel him swell within my mouth right before he releases.

"Come here." His hands pull on my shoulders, urging me up.

I crawl slowly up his body, stopping to twirl my tongue around his right nipple. It draws a faint moan from his lips.

"Sit on me, Bell."

I straddle his groin, rubbing my wetness against him. I reach down to grab hold of him, guiding the tip of his hardness over my clit.

"No," He shifts his hips beneath me. "Christ, don't do that. I'll come just from that."

I smile as I lean forward to kiss him deeply. I rest myself against him, feeling how thick and hard he is. I've never been with a man his size.

His hand drops to my ass. He rubs it gently before he reaches forward to pull his fingers through my folds again. "You're so wet. It's so good."

I run my tongue over his bottom lip and down his chin as I inch my body back, giving him the access he needs to slide himself into me.

We gasp in unison the moment the tender head of his cock brushes against my folds. I cry out as I feel him push my hips down and I feel a rush of tears when he slams his body up and into me.

"Ah, fuck, yes," he purrs. "You're so goddamn tight. Fuck. It's so good."

I lean forward to rest my cheek against his. "It's so much, Caleb."

He kisses my lips tenderly and softly and before I have time to process what is happening, he's flipped us over. He moves forward slightly, pulsing his hips until his cock is buried balls deep within me.

I moan not only from the pleasure but also from the bite of pain that comes with every thrust. I try to say his name. I want to say something but the only thing I can do is feel.

He pumps himself into me, finding a steady pace quickly. My body tightens with every movement, grabbing hold of his thickness, taking everything it can from him.

He says my name over and over with each breath he takes. I cling to him, feeling things I've never felt before. I sense myself falling closer to the edge of an intense orgasm each time he pumps the wide head of his cock deeper within me. He moves slightly, grabbing hold of my hip so he can adjust the angle of his movements.

I cry out as I feel the heat bearing down on me. I look up into his face and his eyes are wide, wild and focused completely on my face. I part my lips, suck in a deep breath and come with a deep and unfamiliar growl.

He ups the tempo, drives his cock into me and fucks me hard and fast until he finds his own release.

* * *

"I'll have to let you go one day."

I don't want those to be the first words I hear when I wake in his arms. I want those words to be part of a nightmare that I've just had and when I actually open my eyes, Caleb will tell me that he can't bear the thought of not being with me.

"Quiet," I say as I tap him on his chest. "Just don't."

"Rowan." He shifts us both until I'm on my back again.

I know that if I open my eyes he'll be hovering above me. I'll have to look up into his beautiful face and listen to him tell me that we can't make this work. I don't want to hear that right now. I've just had the most incredible experience of my entire life. I've felt pleasure that I didn't even know existed and now the man that I shared that with is eager to tell me why it's only a temporary thing.

"Open your eyes." I feel his fingers brush against my lips. "Open them."

I reluctantly look up into his face. We'd both fallen asleep after we came. I'd listened to the sounds of his breathing for more than an hour before I rested my head against his chest and fell into a deep sleep. It feels as though only minutes have passed since he was inside of me but I suspect it is hours later by now.

He pushes a breath out between his lips. "That was more perfect than I ever imagined it would be."

I smile softly as I reach up to cup his cheek in my hand. "It was incredible, Caleb."

"Asher told me you were here." He leans down to brush his lips across my brow. "He told me you were alone and I had to come."

"You saw him?" I ask with a sense of relief. "I was scared that he wouldn't make it back. I was worried that he'd take off again."

"He made it back. He came back because of you."

As much as I'd love to take credit for Asher's return to New York, I can't. "He went back because it was time."

"It doesn't matter why he's back." His voice is low and stoic. "He's back and I'll get the chance I wanted to show him what he means to me."

I close my eyes, wanting the world to melt away and hoping that the tender and compassionate side of Caleb that I'm seeing now is here to stay.

THIRTY-EIGHT

I moan from the strong taste of his flesh. I look up into his face but he's lost in his pleasure. He's standing against the window, his hands wrapped tightly in my hair.

He'd gotten up to look out the window when he thought I was still asleep. I'd silently crawled out of bed behind him and slid my hands around his waist, cupping his heavy balls in one hand while I stroked his cock with the other. He'd moaned when I dropped to my knees and begged him to turn around.

Now, I'm naked, aroused and craving the taste of his release.

"Fuck, yes." He pushes the words out in the middle of a deep growl. "Take it deeper."

I push myself forward, sliding more of the thick vein between my lips. I stroke it quickly with both hands, marveling at how much it pulses beneath my touch.

One of his hands moves to the back of my head as the other finds the windowsill. "I have to fuck your mouth. I have to."

I feel my sex ache with the lust that is woven into his words. I nod slowly while I look up into his face. I want to tell him to do it, but I can't stop myself. I crave the taste of his cock.

He starts pumping his hips slowly, moaning loudly with each thrust.

I pull away from him so I can lick the entire length up and down. I do it slowly, methodically and when I reach the base, I circle my tongue around it. I want to tease him and pull him as close to the edge of his orgasm as I can.

"Fuck, Bell." His words contain every bit as much desire as his body does. He pulls my hair, until my mouth is back at the wide, spongy crown. "Take it all."

I part my lips a touch but his impatience takes control and in one quick and lust filled movement he's pushing my head down, forcing his cock down my throat. My eyes water with the sheer girth of it but I don't stop. I grab hold of it again and pump it until I finally feel his body tense before the first burst of hot, thick release hits the back of my throat.

* * *

"I want to know about the chef."

I look over to where he's standing by the foot of the bed. He's fully dressed now. I'd showered after he came in my mouth and on my face. He'd wanted to taste me again but I needed a chance to breathe. I'd felt overwhelmed by the depth of our intimacy and the shower gave me the brief reprieve that I needed.

"What chef?" I brush past him to pull a pair of panties from the drawer I'd put them in when I unpacked. I choose a black lace pair and pull them on while he stares at me.

"I heard you talking to Clive about a guy one day when I came to your office. You said he was gorgeous and that he's a chef." His eyes slide over my bare breasts before they settle on my face. "Is he the guy you were going to have dinner with? Did that happen?"

The conversation feels foreign to me given the fact that we'd just spent the day sharing ourselves with each other. "Why are you talking about this now?"

He rubs his hand over his chin. "We should talk about what we expect from each other when we get back to New York."

No. We shouldn't talk about that because I don't want to hear him tell me that he's going to fuck other women when I can still taste his desire on my lips.

"Now?" I spit back as I pull a black t-shirt over my head. "Why now?"

His feet shuffle over the floor as he scrubs his hand over the back of his neck. "Things are different now. Everything is different between us now."

"I'm not seeing anyone. I don't have any plans to see anyone."

"What about the chef?"

"I've never met him. I don't know anything about him," I half-lie. I had done a quick Google search of his name when Ivy first told me about him. He's handsome, in an unkempt, dark haired, tattooed and sexy as all hell kind of way. He's making big waves in the culinary world and he's dating up a storm.

From the images I saw online of him coming out of virtually every hot club in New York the past few months, a quick fuck is all that's on his menu. It would definitely be a fun experience but the emotional fall out from that isn't something I have time for. Tyler Monroe may have been someone I'd want to hook up with a few months ago, but my feelings are so jumbled around Caleb now, that I can't see past that.

"Caleb." I rest both of my hands against his chest. "I'm not going to go on a date with him. I'm not planning on dating anyone after what happened between us."

"I don't…I'm not sure…Bell…," he stammers as his eyes search my face. "I'm not sure we should only…I didn't think about us just seeing each other."

I close my eyes willing him to shut his goddamn mouth. "Stop. Just don't say it."

"I think we should talk about it now. It's importan"Are you going to see other women when we get back to New York?"

"I don't know. I don't know what I'm going to do."

I won't cry. I'm not going to let him break me apart. "Do you regret what we did?"

"No." He grabs hold of my biceps, shaking me slightly. "I wanted that. I still want that. I want that and I want you to be my friend."

"I don't understand," I say because there's nothing else. "We can be lovers and friends. You know that we can be both, right?"

"I can't stand the thought of us hurting each other. I don't want that to happen and if we keep fucking each other we will. It will kill me inside if I break your heart." His hands drop to his sides before he turns and walks out of the room.

It's all I need to hear. My life changing long weekend in the Hamptons just came to a screeching, painful halt.

THIRTY-NINE

I told you so.

It's one of those things that you never want to hear anyone saying to you. It's degrading and emotionally debilitating. It's also a blunt reminder of how foolish you are. Once I walk through the door of my apartment, I expect Graham to be standing there with a bright neon sign with the words, '*I told you so,*' written across it in big, bold letters.

I swallow my pride as I push open the door. He's right there, pulling me into a tight embrace before I even have time to explain the cryptic text I sent him an hour ago telling him that I'd been with Caleb but I was coming home early to hide in my bed.

"You look like hell, Rowan." He takes hold of my purse and my suitcase. "You should sit down. I can make you something to eat."

"No." I shake my head. "I'm not hungry."

"Do you want to take a bath?" He leads me to a chair in the living room. "I'll go get it ready for you."

He'll do it without question. I know that he will. I also know that he'll sit next to the tub and listen while I weep about how wonderful it felt to be wanted by Caleb only to turn around and hear him tell me that he wants to keep his options open.

Graham will ask what lesson I've learned from the weekend and the only thing I can honestly offer is that I can't take showers when I'm around Caleb. I go in thinking he desires me more than any woman he's ever met and I come out to find him second guessing everything we share.

"I don't want to take a bath." I pat the arm of the chair. "Sit here with me."

I lower myself into the chair as he takes a seat next to me. I look up into his kind face. I had thought about having the driver take me to Ivy's apartment but trying to explain all of this to her right now feels overwhelming. I know that Graham doesn't expect anything from me other than what I can give. Right now, I'm not sure that's much more than silence.

"I wish I could tell you that I'd gone through this too but I don't have any friends who I knew when I was a kid." He taps my shoulder. "I grew out of those friendships when I got older. We didn't have anything in common anymore."

"You don't think you could want someone you grew up with?"

"None of the boys I played with when I was a kid would be open to playing with me in the way I want now," he says with a wink. "I'm not convinced that being friends first is the way to go."

I would have argued that point with him at one time but after I'd gotten dressed and told Caleb I wanted to go back to New York, I have no choice but to agree with Graham's philosophy on the subject. Caleb hadn't argued with me. He didn't try to explain anything. He simply called for a car, and sent me on my way, telling me that he'd hang back to close up the house.

"I think he has issues," I say before I realize how open ended that sounds. "I mean I feel as though he's in a constant battle with himself over me, or maybe it's over us. He just seems so passionate and loving one minute and then it all shifts."

"Has Caleb ever been in love?"

I hate to admit it, especially now given the fact that Vena was close to becoming his wife. She was a model who he met at a photo shoot for the woman's clothing line. He'd fallen for her so fast that soon after his brothers and I met her, there was a beautiful canary diamond on her finger. He secured the most sought after wedding planner in the city, chose the venue and planned a life with her. It was her choice to end the relationship. Maybe that's where it all stems from. Maybe he's still head over heels crazy in love with her.

"Once." I hold up my left hand and wiggle my ring finger. "They were engaged. She broke it off before the wedding."

"Ah."

I wait in silence for something more and there's absolutely nothing. "That's it? Do you think the hot and cold bullshit he pulls on me has to do with her? You must have an opinion."

"You know I do." He skims his hand over my hair. "Are you sure you want to hear it?"

I'm not sure but I know I have to hear it. I've replayed what happened in the bedroom of the Hamptons house over and over again since

I left there. None of it makes sense to me. "I need to hear it."

"Caleb loves you as much, if not more, than he loved the woman he was engaged to." He cups his hand under my chin. "He's so scared that you're going to break his heart that he's determined to break yours first."

I shake my head slightly, noting the resistance in his touch. "I don't think that's it. If Caleb loved me he'd tell me. He wouldn't push me away."

"The fact that he's pushing you away is his way of telling you he loves you, Rowan. He's scared and he doesn't know how to trust in his own heart."

FORTY

"Are you planning on going to that party the Fosters are having?"

I came into work a day earlier than I had originally planned. It's Tuesday morning and the first words out of Clive's mouth are about the Foster family. I may just need to pack up my life and move to California to escape those men.

"No," I say without asking any details about what the hell he's talking about. The very last thing I want to do right now is party with the Fosters. I'd rather do my taxes, or Clive's taxes or anyone's taxes.

"No?" he repeats back. "You're not planning on sending Jordan in your place, are you?"

My eyes dart up to his face. I can't tell if he's being sarcastic or not. The Jordan joke is past its prime but Clive is notorious for beating a joke to death with the hope that he can get one final laugh out of it. "If the Foster brothers are having a party, I don't want to be there."

"You need to be there," he says succinctly. "It's a charity event, Rowan. I'm presenting the Foundation with a gift from Corteck and since Lilly's best friend is Ben Foster we need to have a strong presence at the event."

Dr. Ben Foster is one of the few Fosters I've yet to meet. He's Caleb, Asher and Gabriel's cousin. He's also co-founder of the Foster Foundation with his twin brother Noah, the famed photographer. I met Noah four years ago when I went to a private showing of one of his gallery openings. The walls had been covered with breathtaking photographs of nude women. I was in awe of his talent and mesmerized by his passion to create art. We'd had a long conversation about chasing after your dreams and even though my dreams didn't line up with his, he was encouraging and attentive.

"There's no reason for me to be there," I point out. "I admire everything the Foundation does, but it has nothing to do with me."

It's true. The Foster Foundation is an organization that provides medical care to anyone who can't afford it. The main focus has always been on providing for those who have no roof over their heads. Ben Foster has set up clinics around the city for anyone who wants care but can't pay for it. Their philosophy is simple. They don't ask questions. They are there to help. I've gifted their non-profit with a check for the past two years on my birthday as a way to celebrate my own good health.

"Corteck is partnering with the Foundation." He lowers himself into one of the chairs in front of my desk. "We're donating a software program that the city's homeless shelters can use to streamline the medical care of the people who stay at those facilities."

Again, I don't see the direct connection to me. "That's great, Clive. You know I'm on board for anything philanthropic that the company does, but I'm sure someone else can take my place."

"I'm not asking you to be there as an employee, Rowan." He crosses his legs as he leans forward in the chair. "I'm asking you as a friend. This is a big deal to Lilly and I."

I need to widen my circle of friends beyond people with the surname Foster, but until I manage that, I have to do the right thing. "Tell me when and where, and I'll be there."

* * *

"I didn't know if you'd stop by." Asher swings the door of his apartment open.

I scan his face noting how much different he looks now that he's shaved the beard and had his hair cut. He looks exactly as he did before he ran away on his selfish adventure. I'm still reeling from the realization that he was so close and yet couldn't find it within himself to send any one of us a text saying he was alive and fine.

"I'm glad you called," I say honestly. I was grateful to see his number pop up on my phone this morning as I was walking through the lobby of the Corteck building to my office. I've been back from the Hamptons for three days now and even though I've been tempted to call Caleb, I haven't done it.

"How long can you stay?"

Considering it's the middle of the day and I've fallen behind on my work, I'm given myself just an hour to hear Asher out. "I should be back at the office by three."

He nods. "I've been doing a lot of thinking since I got back. I've thought about my brothers and you too, Bell."

I don't look at him as I take a seat on a white leather chair that faces the bank of windows that overlook midtown Manhattan.

Asher's apartment may not be as openly extravagant as either of his brothers' places, but it's still located in one of the most sought after buildings in the city. The view alone is worth the steep price of a bachelor apartment on this block.

"I let all of you down." He pulls on the legs of his black pants before he takes a seat in the chair next to me. "I let myself down too."

I turn my head towards him. "You did let us down."

"I know." He gazes over the city's skyline. "I should have stayed and talked to Caleb or Gabriel. I could have talked to you."

I rub my hand over the front of my neck, my fingers catching on the thin silver necklace I'm wearing. "Your brothers wanted to help you."

His jaw tightens. "I felt overwhelmed by everything. I needed an escape and I thought about shooting up."

"You didn't, did you?" I ask quietly.

"No. I'll never do that again." He reaches to pull my hand into his. "I lost something that day I was arrested, Bell. Something that meant everything to me and instead of dealing with it, I ran. I hid. I handled it wrong."

I stare at him, startled by the admission. "What did you lose that day?"

"My son." His hand falls from mine. "I lost my son that morning."

FORTY-ONE

Neither of us says a word as we stare out the window at the rain pelting against the glass. The entire mood of the city changes when a storm approaches. It shifts from a vibrant, beautiful place to a dark, disjointed rush of bodies all moving quickly to find shelter. I love the rain. I've always found comfort in the fact that it washes away everything in its path. I need that now. Asher does too.

"I met a woman in rehab," he finally speaks. "Her name was Karen. I thought I loved her."

I struggle with what to say. "Caleb told me you two were married briefly."

He doesn't flinch at the words so I know he's already aware of how much information his brother had uncovered about the parts of his life he's been hiding from all of us. "It was only a few weeks. I knew once I was done with the program and in therapy that it wasn't a real bond. I didn't love her the way she needed me to."

"How did she feel about you?"

"She hated me," he chuckles softly. "She loved me. She didn't want to let me go."

I study his profile. The contours of his face have changed since he became a man. There's still softness in his jawline and youthfulness in his eyes. I'm only a year older than him but I've always felt as though he was much younger than me.

He turns abruptly to look directly at me. "She was pregnant. We were together once after we both got out of rehab and she got pregnant."

"When did you find out?" I still.

"A couple of months ago," he says regretfully. "She'd been trying to contact me for weeks but I ignored her calls and texts. She came by the office one day and I had security remove her without even talking to her."

I look back at the wet city. "What happened that day? The day you were arrested?"

He scrubs his hand over his brow. "I'd seen her the day before to talk about custody and money. She wanted something in place before the baby arrived."

I don't say anything. I don't want to derail what he's feeling or sharing.

"Her doctor suggested an amniocentesis because of her drug use." He shakes his head as he rests his elbows on his knees. "I wouldn't have cared if there was anything wrong with him. I would have taken care of him."

The emotion in his voice is all the proof anyone would need of how desperately Asher loved that baby. "I know you would have."

He nods as his eyes lock on mine. "All of those tests came back fine. He's a healthy baby."

I smile even though I'm caught in a circle of confusion. "What happened to the baby, Asher?"

"My attorney wanted me to request paternity testing." He shrugs his shoulder. "I asked Karen and she refused so we got a court order."

"The baby isn't…"

"He's not," he interrupts me. "I got the call that morning that the results were in so I went to pick them up and that's what it said. There's zero chance I'm the father."

"I'm sorry." I say unsure of what I can add that will offer anything in the form of comfort. "I'm really sorry."

He looks at me with both brows raised. "That news changed my life, Bell. It made me realize how much I want to be a dad."

It's the silver lining he needs to find to make the situation feel okay. I get that. He used to do it when we were in college too and he'd failed a class or bomb a test. The positive is what always pulls him through.

"I came to your office the morning after I was arrested to tell you." He slides his fingers against the glass of the window. "I couldn't do it. I couldn't say the words out loud."

"I'm glad you told me now."

"Me too," he says roughly. "You deserve to know what pushed me to run."

I clasp my hands together in my lap, wanting to reach out to embrace him but knowing that he needs to find his own strength within. "How are you feeling now?"

"I'm going back to therapy. I'm working on my music too." He taps his fingers on the arm of the chair. "I need to grow up. I want to be a good husband and father one day. That's my goal. If I can have that, I'll have everything."

FORTY-TWO

"You look beautiful, Rowan."

I don't want to turn around. It's the first time I've heard his voice since I left the house in the Hamptons. I've tried to busy myself with work but it's been useless.

I hear my office door close and I know that he's standing in the small space with me. I smooth my hands over the navy skirt that I'm wearing. I'd gotten up extra early today and had headed to a yoga class to try and work off some of the unbearable tension I feel throughout my body. I had hoped that it would offer me an escape from the emotional abyss I've been floating in. When I was done there, I felt just as tied up in knots as I had before, so I'd hit the gym. By the time I'd taken my body to its limits, I had only a few minutes to ready myself for work. I'd showered quickly before I ran a comb through my hair and pulled on the skirt and a light blue short sleeved sweater. I look like I feel inside; tousled and weary.

"Caleb," I whisper his name as I pivot on my heel to face him. "Why are you here?"

He's sharply dressed in a dark grey suit. His hair is combed, his face shaved. He looks as though he just spent a week at a spa enjoying tropical drinks and long massages. "I wanted to talk."

Of course he did. He decided to show his face again when he'd gathered up the emotional strength to finally look me in the eye.

"How have you been?" he asks hoarsely.

I stare at him. It's a question you ask someone you spot on the street that you haven't seen in years. It's a generic greeting meant to fill in the empty space between two people who have nothing left to say to one another. It's not the words a man says to a woman after he's claimed her body and brought her more pleasure than she can absorb.

"How have I been? I repeat back with my brow furrowed. "How have I been?"

He rakes his hand through his hair. "Bell, please. I fucked up. I really fucked up."

"Do you know how I've felt?" My hand trembles as I reach for my chest. "Do you know how deep the ache is that is inside of me?"

His eyes follow the path of my hand. "I know. I feel it. It's inside of me too."

It can't be. If it was, he would have come to my apartment days ago and swept me into his arms. If he felt the same loss and longing that I do, he would have called to tell me that he was sorry. He wouldn't have waited almost an entire week to show up in the middle of the day at my office.

"You pull me close and then you push me away." My hands fly into the air between us, mimicking a pushing motion. "You want me, and then you don't. You fuck me, and then you leave. You can't do it. You can't do that to me."

He moves one step closer. The scent of his cologne wafts through the air as he leans down to look into my eyes. "I have wanted you since I can remember. I have fucked other women to try and forget about you. I asked a woman to marry me so I could kill the need that is inside of me for you. I have been living with this need for my entire life. It never goes away. Ever."

His words hit me with such a force that I stumble on my feet. I have to reach for the side of my desk to steady my balance. "You don't mean that."

"You can't see it." He reaches out to grab hold of my hand. "You've never been able to see it."

He's wrong. I've seen glimpses of desire over the years but they've always been fleeting. "Why haven't you told me before now?"

He rubs his fingers over the top of his lip. "When you were a senior in college I made a trip to see you."

I can't push my mind back to that place right now. "I don't remember."

"It was during semester break." He reaches towards me, brushing his fingers against my cheek. "Asher had sent me a picture of the two of you. God, you looked amazing. Your hair was pinned on top of your head and you were staring right at the camera."

I wish I could remember the image. Asher had taken hundreds of pictures in college to document his time there. I'd made him delete dozens because he'd caught me, and many of my friends, off guard.

"I'm sorry. I can't remember what picture that is."

"I'll never forget that photograph." He throws his head back briefly before he looks at me again. "I came to tell you that I couldn't stop thinking about you. I knew you were set to graduate and I was panicked that since you weren't accepting our job offer, that you'd take a position across the country or on the other side of the world."

"So you came to see me?" I know I sound utterly confused because that's exactly how I feel. I remember virtually every conversation I've ever had with him. I don't remember seeing him during semester break of my senior year.

"I did." He rubs the pad of his thumb across my bottom lip. "I wanted to kiss you so badly. I had it all planned out."

"You didn't?" I can't contain a smile.

His tongue darts out over his lips. "I had planned to tell Asher to have you standing in a spot where you'd see me approaching across the quad."

I nod silently.

"You'd see me and you'd wave and as I got closer, you'd realize that I was holding that stuffed bear you used to sleep with when you came to the house in the Hamptons. I still have that thing in my apartment."

My eyes fill with tears. As much as I don't want to cry, I can't quell the emotional roller coaster I feel myself riding. "You have it?"

He cradles my cheek in his palm. "You'd see the bear and you'd see my face and you'd feel everything that I feel close my eyes wanting the world to whisk me back to that day.

"That never happened. I was never on the quad with Asher."

"When I called to tell him that I was coming, he told me about Tom." He swallows hard. "He told me you were in love and happy. He said you were so happy."

I was. I thought I was. I did love Tom as much as I could before I realized that his addictions would always be his first love. "I was happy then."

"I went to Europe so I wouldn't get in the way." His eyes wander to the wall behind me. "I wanted to come there and tell you that he was wrong for you, but I couldn't do that, Bell. I called and wished you and Tom well instead because I just wanted to hear your voice. It killed me that I missed my chance."

I stare at him while I try to piece together the disjointed pieces of that time in my life. Tom and I were planning our future then. We'd already started looking at apartments. I believed he was my happily-ever-after until months later when I truly understood the depth of his dependence on cocaine.

"I met Vena right after that," he says quietly. "I hooked up with her because she filled an empty spot."

"You loved her. You were going to marry her." I drop my gaze to the floor.

"I don't think I ever really loved her." His chest expands as he pulls in a deep breath. "I used her to forget about you."

FORTY-THREE

When Tom left me, I wanted Caleb. I can't pretend that isn't my reality. I met a man right after the break up and I slept with him on our second date just so I could feel something. The entire time I was in bed with him, Caleb was in my thoughts. I didn't close my eyes and imagine it was Caleb fucking me. That wouldn't have worked even if I wanted it to. The man didn't look like him, he smelled nothing like Caleb and the size of his body wasn't comparable in the least, but he did give me something I needed. He took me to a place for a little more than an hour where my emotional pain ceased to exist. I was grateful and we dated a few times after that but it didn't fill the void that Tom left.

When all that dust settled, and I was finally alone, I wanted to talk to Caleb. I called him and instead of returning my call, he'd come to see me. The very first words out of his mouth were about Vena. He brought her to meet me the very next day. He looked content and excited and when he left my apartment with her, I'd cried not for the loss of what could have been. It wasn't about that. Back then I was mourning the loss of my own dream of being with Tom and Caleb's apparent happiness only punctuated the pain I was already in.

"You were happy when you told me that you were getting married." My arms wrap around my waist. I'm trying to shelter myself. I feel it. "You were planning your wedding."

"I was fond of Vena," he admits as he shuffles on his feet. "She was fun and carefree. I'd never met anyone like her before."

I hadn't probed Caleb for any details about his fiancé at the time but Asher was overflowing with information. He told me that his brother and Vena had a passionate affair that ended when he returned to the States. According to Asher, they missed each other so much that Caleb arranged for her to fly to New York to live with him. It was fast, intense and within just a few months, they were engaged.

"She was beautiful," I begin before I stop to correct myself. "She is beautiful. I only met her that one time but I've seen pictures of her online."

"I haven't seen her in years." He takes a step back before he bends his legs to lower himself into one of the chairs in front of my desk. "I don't keep in touch with her."

"How did it end?" It's a question that has been haunting me since he showed up at my apartment that night after the engagement was called off. "She ended it?"

"Yes." He frowns. "We argued about everything. Where to live, when to have children, what color to paint the foyer; we couldn't agree on anything anymore."

"I know it was hard for you."

He glances briefly at my desk and the bouquet of flowers I bought myself on my way to work yesterday. "Losing Vena wasn't hard. I didn't miss her after we ended things."

"You were upset," I say wearily. "You were upset for months."

"She broke emotionally when she found out I was fucking someone else." He grazes his hand over his chin. "We ended things on a Friday and Saturday night I was in bed with a woman I met at a club."

I'm taken back by the admission. "That's fast."

"Physically, maybe." He half-shrugs. "Emotionally I had checked out of the relationship with Vena months before."

"I didn't know that it had gotten that bad between you."

He crosses his legs as he looks up at me. "I thought that if I married her, I'd satisfy something within me. Part of it was pressure from my mother. She adored Vena and still does. I guess another part of it was my need to fulfill Vena's dreams since she'd helped me overcome a lot of my own bullshit. I pushed aside all of the doubt I was feeling to give it a chance. I was a ticking time bomb. It really fell apart right when we were making plans for the wedding."

"You never told me about any of this." I'm not being accusatory. My relationship with Caleb has always had an ebb and flow to it that neither of us completely understood. There were so many complicated facets to it that I've always just accepted it for what it is.

"Vena was a mess after we split." His breath hisses out between clenched teeth. "I hate talking about this but she fell apart. It took her months to finally get back on her feet and she still hates me to this day."

"You're not responsible for that." I want to sound comforting but that's not how it sounds at all. "Vena handled the break up in her own way."

"She loved me, Rowan." His voice is raw. "She loved me and I let her down."

FORTY-FOUR

"I'm not her, Caleb."

The angle of his face changes. He tilts his head gently to the left so his eyes catch mine. "You're nothing like her."

"You think I'll fall apart the way she did?" I cross my legs at the ankles as I lean back against my desk. "You're scared that I'll be destroyed if things don't work out between us?"

His left brow arches as he considers the question. He pauses before he answers. "No. It's not just that."

I should probably point out that he's wasted the past fifteen minutes of his life explaining his relationship to Vena to me if it has no bearing on his reluctance to let the emotional barriers he's built around himself down. "What is it then? Why do you pull back every time we get close?"

"It's me," he continues, "I'm more like Vena than you are. If things don't work out between us, we'll both be destroyed."

I can't argue with him. I've had a taste of the pain that is born from being rejected by him and it's deep and unrelenting. "It hurts me when you push me away."

A flash of something unfamiliar darts over his expression. He winces slightly before he clears his throat. "I fucked up after we made love. I really fucked up."

"I wanted to talk about things." I realize how pathetic that sounds, but I don't care. I'm not trying to impress a man I just met. I'm not trying to be strong for the sake of saving my self-esteem. This is Caleb and me. If I can't be brutally honest with him, we'll never have a chance.

"I came to the house so I could fuck you," he growls softly as he says the words. "I was in the house for hours before I came to your room."

"What?"

"I got there in the middle of the night. I let myself in." He stretches his legs out in front of him. "I watched you sleeping. I was so hard."

"I had no clue you were there."

"You were fast asleep and then you got up." He smiles softly. "Christ, I almost grabbed you in the hallway when you walked out of the bedroom."

"You were watching me? You just stood there watching me?"

His shoulders slouch forward. "I was mesmerized. It felt like time had stopped and I was breathing for the first time."

I don't say anything. I can't. My ability to speak has vanished because of the pressure of my emotions within my chest.

"Then you went back to bed and I came into the room," he rasps. "I couldn't control my need anymore. I stood there, willing you to wake back up and when you did I saw it in your face. I saw how much you wanted me."

I'd be wasting my energy trying to deny that. I had been just as eager to taste his lips again as he had been to taste mine. My lust had ruled each and every movement I made that morning and I don't regret any of it. I finally got to have the one man I've longed for my entire life.

"I've never been with a man like you," I confess quietly. "I've never felt those things before."

He's on his feet so quickly, his mouth pressing tenderly over mine. I grab hold of his hands as they cup my cheeks.

"I want to try, Bell," he whispers the words softly against my lips. "I want to try and give you everything you need."

My heart stalls. "You can't push me away if it's too much. You need to talk to me."

"I'm scared," he admits as he rests his forehead against mine. "I'll hurt myself before I'll cause you pain."

"I won't let that happen." I glide my mouth over his again. I will do everything in my power to not let it happen. I'll fight with all that I am to make certain that Caleb and I get the chance at happiness we deserve.

FORTY-FIVE

"Judging by all that lipstick on Caleb Foster's mouth, I'm guessing you're now going to the benefit dinner as his date."

When Clive knocked on my office door a few minutes ago, I'd told Caleb that I had work to do. I do. I need to finish some things before the end of the day and I also need time to absorb what just happened. When dreams finally come true there should be a mandatory adjustment period that comes with them.

"We didn't talk about that," I say sheepishly. I study a file folder that's on my desk completely oblivious to what it contains.

"It looks like you didn't talk at all," he murmurs. "This doesn't mean you're abandoning us to go work for them, does it?"

"At Foster Enterprises?" I chuckle softly as I ask the question. "I'm a Corteck girl through and through. I'd never go to work for Caleb and his brothers."

He plays with his wedding ring. "You know I wish my wife worked here with us. It's a bone of contention in our marriage."

"Really?" I lean my elbows on the desk. Lilly and Clive have an exceptional relationship. They may not have started down the rosy path towards bliss with everything working for them, but they managed to jump over many hurdles to find a way to make it work. "I thought you were all for her working with Alec Hughes."

Alec Hughes is admittedly our biggest competition in the tech world. He runs his own company that is housed just a few blocks from here. Clive and he are old friends and equally old adversaries. When Lilly left Corteck to work for Alec, I tried desperately to get her to come back. I knew it meant a lot to Clive and since Lilly is one of the best programmers in the game today, it's been a loss that all of us have deeply felt.

"You know that Foster is opening a new line of lingerie boutiques, right?"

I only know that from getting a Google news alert about it. The boutiques carry high end, designer lingerie. The press release touted the name of the line as Loire. It's a new brand for the family to nurture, which typically means they'll be fighting over which one of them will handle the reins.

"I read about it." I flip open my laptop cover. "It seems like a smart move on their part."

He cocks a dark brow. "You think it's a smart move because it plays into the women's brand they've already established."

"That," I begin before I stop to lean back in my chair. "It's not only that. The Fosters know how to sell what women crave. They'll create a demand for it and women will rush to have Loire lingerie."

"You're sure you're not gearing up to be the divisional manager of that?"

I laugh out loud. "No one has approached me. They're not going to. Caleb knows exactly how much I love my job here."

* * *

"Rowan Bell?" The dark haired woman repeats my name again. "You work for Gabriel Foster, don't you?"

Um, no. I do not work for Gabriel or anyone with the surname Foster.

"I'm here to see Caleb Foster." I look past her to the offices that house Gabriel and Caleb's employees. Normally I'd stroll right past this desk because the woman who generally sits here knows exactly who I am. This woman, who appears to have just started working here, judging by the ultra-tidy desk she's sitting behind, has no clue that I'm an old family friend.

"You're not here to see Gabriel?" Her lips thin into a frown.

I fish in my purse for my phone. I could have called Caleb to tell him to come out to the reception area to get me by now. "I know Gabriel, but I'm here to see Caleb."

"So you're telling me that Gabriel is an acquaintance of yours, but you'd rather talk to his brother?"

I pinch the bridge of my nose to ward off the headache that is charging at me at full speed. "Can you please tell Caleb that Rowan is here?"

"Shall I also tell Gabriel that you're here in the event that he has something to discuss with you?"

I shake my head as I press the call button on my smartphone. I listen to the ring of Caleb's phone in my ear and also in the distance. He's not answering.

"Are you calling Caleb?" She turns to face his office. "I heard that. You were calling Caleb, weren't you?"

Who hires the people that work here?

"Can you see if Asher is in?" I ask knowing that there's a very real, and distinct, possibility that her head will pop off.

"Wait." She drops the pen she's been holding in her hand even though she hasn't written anything down since I exited the elevator and walked up to her desk. "You want to see Asher now?"

"Just find me a Foster," I spit the words out. "Any of them will do."

FORTY-SIX

"I've never fucked anyone in my office before." His hands are above me as he pushes my body against the wall.

"I once fucked…"

"Jesus, Rowan." His head dips down so his lips touch mine. "Don't ever tell me about fucking another man."

I reach up to guide his face so I can seal my mouth over his. He moans into our kiss as his hands slide down to grab hold of the hem of my skirt. I came here to talk to him about the Foster Foundation benefit but I knew the moment he came into Gabriel's office to get me after his meeting, that I'd be lost in his touch before I left the building.

He'd pulled me into his office before he slammed the door behind us quickly. His suit jacket was on the floor in seconds, followed by his tie. I was unbuttoning his shirt when he cursed under his breath, pinned me to the wall and started kissing me.

"Do you have a condom?" I tug on his belt. "You have condoms in your wallet, right?"

"No." His hands inch up my thighs. "I don't carry condoms around with me."

"You don't?" I don't even try and mask the surprise in my voice. "I can't believe you don't carry condoms with you."

He's amused. The ghost of a grin that floats over his full lips gives it away. "Why is that so unbelievable?"

I wrap my hands around his neck, rubbing my index finger on the bottom of his hairline. "I think you buy a lot of condoms. I just assumed you'd keep them everywhere."

His eyebrows both jump. "Everywhere as in where?"

"The bedroom, obviously, the kitchen, maybe tucked in a corner of the library if the mood strikes you." I tap my finger against the base of his neck with each place I ramble off. "Also, in the back of that car that drives you around the city, your gym bag, and of course, your wallet."

"That's a lot of places." His tongue juts out and traces a path over my bottom lip.

"I know you like to have sex." It didn't sound quite as juvenile as that when it popped into my mind. "I mean, you were talking about sex with a woman a few weeks ago on the phone when you called me to your apartment."

Tilting his head he kisses me softly. "I think I was interviewing Ruby on the phone that day."

I laugh loudly, throwing my neck back so violently with joy that my head hits the wall with a loud thump." You were not talking to Ruby about sex that day."

"Oh?" His hand reaches up to rub the back of my skull. "Ruby made it very clear when I hired her that I could use her in any way I want."

I grimace at both the thought of that proposition and the lump that is now growing on the back of my scalp. "We're not fucking other people, right?"

"There's no one in this room but me and you." His hands both drop to my skirt again.

I inch my legs apart, willing his fingers to my core so he can feel how wet I am. "You know what I mean."

"I don't want you to touch another man, Bell." His lips sweep across my neck. "I don't want any other woman."

"You're all mine?" I whisper the words softly. "Tell me you're all mine."

"I'm all yours," he says as he drops to his knees, pulls my panties aside and tongues me until I fall into his arms.

* * *

"I thought we were going to fuck." I adjust my skirt and blouse.

He rakes his hand through his now messy hair. "Why does my cock get hard as soon as I hear you say that word?"

"Fuck?" I don't turn in his direction as I reach into my purse to retrieve my lipstick.

"When did you start saying that?" He's beside me now, taking the slender case from my fingers. I stand in silence as he twists the tube, pulling the nude lipstick into view. He carefully applies it to my mouth.

"I started saying it when I started doing it. I mean I don't say it to men, or any of the men I've been with. Just you." I pucker my lips together. "Do my lips look nice?"

"Christ." He shakes his head as he drops the tube back in my purse. "You may be the most sensual woman I've ever met."

"Me?" My hand leaps to my chest and I realize my bra is peeking out of the top of my blouse. "I'm not that sensual."

He adjusts the top of my shirt, carefully folding the fabric over so it hides the lace of my bra. "That's what makes you so hot, Bell. You don't even know what you do to men."

That's actually very true. I know the fundamentals of what to do to a man when we're both naked. Outside the bedroom, when it comes to the allure of seduction, I'm like a doe that is lost in the woods. I've always just been myself and that's worked for me.

"Back to my original comment," I say before I bend over to adjust the strap of my shoe. "Why didn't you make love to me?"

"I want the next time I make love to you to be in my bed." He looks down at his watch. "Say, in three hours? Does that work for you?"

"It works." I glide my hand down his cheek. "I'll be there."

FORTY-SEVEN

I arch my back just as his teeth bite into my nipple. The mixture of pure pain and pointed pleasure pulls a deep moan from within me. I'd promised myself before I got to Caleb's apartment that I'd enjoy every single sensation. I want this night to last forever. It's the first time I'm going to spend the night with him. He had insisted on the ride over to his place, from mine, that we'd fall asleep in one another's arms.

He moves slowly across my chest, kissing the soft skin between my breasts. He cups the tender flesh in his hand, rolling it within his palm. "Your breasts are so beautiful. I love how they feel."

I love how he's vocal about my body. I crave the knowledge that it's everything he wants it to be. "Kiss my nipple, Caleb."

His hair tickles my skin as he lowers his mouth to the swollen bud. He kisses it gently at first, before pulling it between his lips. He sucks it, loudly and carefully. I squirm from the feelings it creates in my core. I'm already wet and wanting. I was that way as soon as we'd finished the dinner he'd ordered in for us.

"If I could spend all of my time in this bed with you, I would." He rests his head between my breasts. "I don't need anything in the world but you."

I weave my fingers through his hair. I want to repeat back what he just said but I'm scared. I'm fearful that the promises he made aren't grounded in his real emotions. I'm terrified that when he fucks me tonight, that he'll pull back after just as he did before. My heart can't find the truth in that fear but it's my mind that clutters every thought I'm havHe moves his head again, this time lowering it over my stomach. He trails his lips down my belly, stopping when he reaches my core. He looks up, locking his dark eyes with mine before his tongue darts out and expertly licks at my outer folds.

"I love the taste of you." He nuzzles his face into my wetness. "I need it."

I push my legs apart, not feeling any vulnerability with the movement. I don't care that I'm completely exposed to him. There's no shame in my desire for him. I arch my hips towards him as he dives in and eats me with a fury that screams of the desire he feels for me too.

I open my eyes just as I feel the climax bearing down on me. I crash into it as I see his dark head, moving frantically between my thighs, intent on giving me pleasure. He's focused only on what I need, pushing his own cravings aside.

He reaches for the condom package he had thrown on the bed when we walked into the room. He rips it open quickly and silently. He sheaths his thick cock as his eyes settle on my core.

I cling tightly to him when he inches forward a touch to rub the spongy, wide crown over my clit. He moans when he feels my body tense and he calls out my name when he pushes inside me.

"Rowan," he whispers. "You're everything to me."

I feel the tears burn my cheeks as he finds his rhythm. His thrusts are slow, measured and delicious. He's taking his time. He's pulling as much from this as he's giving.

I whimper when I feel my release. I pull his head down so he can kiss me and he rewards me with a groan wrapped into a sigh.

I come in heated waves; one tormented ripple after another reverberates through every part of me. He stills to watch my face. He stops to hear my cries.

He rolls his hips as he plunges deeper with each heavy thrust and as he finds his own release, tears stream from his eyes and fall onto my chest. My name escapes from between his quivering lips and when he's pumped everything he has into me, he kisses me with a hunger I've never felt before.

FORTY-EIGHT

I walk back into the bedroom after going to find some juice in the kitchen. He'd clung tightly to me after he came. When he finally rolled off me to tie up the condom and toss it in the wastebasket next to the bed, the silence that filled the room was heavy and measured.

I needed to breathe and I needed the hope that would come with hearing him tell me he still wanted me. I'd left to search for a drink to give him time to gather his emotions. I'd witnessed him sob. I'd felt the tears as they hit my skin. I'd wanted to comfort him, and hold him, but he'd brushed his hand across his face and the moment had disappeared without a word.

"My beautiful Bell is back."

The words collapse me from the inside out. I feel my knees buckle beneath me and the glass of orange juice that I'd carefully poured is now spilled all over the floor mixed with the shards of broken glass.

"Be careful." He's on his feet, scooping me up in his arms. "You'll cut your feet."

"I should clean that." I mutter against his chest. "I can get something to clean that up."

"I'll do it." He sets me on the edge of the bed. "I'll go get another glass of juice and then I'll clean it up."

He turns to go and I pull on his elbow to stop him. "No. Don't go."

"I won't." He smiles at me as he tucks my legs beneath the blanket that we just made love on. "Your feet are chilled. You should get under the covers."

I stare at him. I drink in the sight of his flushed skin and the muscular smoothness of his chest. I've always thought of him as the most attractive man I've seen, but now, in the light of the bedroom's lamps and in the glow of my orgasmic high, I see something more. He's not only beautiful to look at. He's kind. It's there in his eyes and in the smile that he reserves for only me.

Caleb Foster is ruthless when it comes to business. He'll take on anyone who threatens what he has built for his family. I've never seen him back down from anything, but tonight I see traces of the boy who used to tease me endlessly.

"I stole one of your sweatshirts."

"I don't have sweatshirts." He tips his chin so his forehead touches mine. "Do I look like a sweatshirt kind of guy to you?"

I tap him on the shoulder. "I'll bet you have sweatshirts. I'll check out your closet."

"You stole some dude's sweatshirt," he teases. "Why the fuck would I let you look in my closet? Do you know how expensive the suits are that are in there?"

I pull my hand over my mouth to stifle the laughter. "You got those suits for free. You own the company that makes them."

"Good point." He furrows his brow in a mock scowl. "Now, back to the clothing that you've been stealing. What's up with that?"

I stretch my legs beneath the sheet, pulling it up higher to cover my breasts. "When we lived next door to each other, I took one of your sweatshirts. You left it hanging on the railing of your stoop."

His breath catches as he brushes his lips over mine. "Why? Why did you take it?"

I kiss him harder before I pull back to rest my cheek against his. "I wanted something of yours for me. I wanted to have it when I slept. I still have it."

"We wasted forever." He strokes his hand over my hair. "We fucking wasted forever."

* * *

"I can't believe you got me a ticket." Graham waves the embossed invitation in the air as if it's the golden ticket to a chocolate factory raffle. "I'm actually going to a Foster Foundation Gala."

"You are." I turn to flash him a smile. "We're both going to sit with Fosters."

"You'll introduce me to all of them, right?" He adjusts the bow tie of the tuxedo he rented. "You do know all of them, don't you?"

"Most of them." I half-shrug as I point to the back of my dress. "Can you zip me?"

I'd chosen a dress from one of the Arilia boutiques. Caleb has no idea that I'm wearing a dress fashioned by one of the company's designers. I paid for it myself because I want to surprise him. I may not see myself working for his family, but I can support them. Wearing this dress to this event is going to show him just how much I treasure my life long connection to him.

"That dress fits you like a glove." Graham motions for me to twirl. "Let me see the entire thing."

I twist around slowly, wanting to make certain he catches me in every angle of the royal blue dress I picked for tonight. "Do you like?"

"I love." He brushes past me. "There's a sapphire necklace in your jewelry drawer. I'm going to grab that."

I don't stop him. I want to look as perfect as I can. Tonight is the night I get to enjoy being Caleb Foster's official date.

FORTY-NINE

"Do you work for Gabriel?" He holds out his hand to gently take mine.

I need to check my social media profiles. Apparently, someone has hacked into them and listed Gabriel Foster as my employer. "I work for Corteck, but I'm an old family friend of the Fosters."

The corner of his mouth slides into a grin. "I'm a Foster."

"No." I laugh nervously. "I'm an old friend of Gabriel, Caleb and Asher."

He points towards where Asher is standing next to his mother. "Then you're a friend of my cousins. I'm Ben."

"You're Dr. Ben Foster," I feel the need to correct him. "You're the founder of the Foster Foundation."

His eyes float towards a beautiful woman standing next to the bar. "My brother, Noah and I are co-founders and my wife, Kayla, she's the brains behind it all."

I know without having to ask that the woman at the bar is Kayla. I can sense it just from the way he looks at her. "I've heard a lot about the Foundation. I think it's an amazing endeavor."

"It's something we started for our mother." His eyes dart to the floor for a brief moment. "She died when we were teenagers. We wanted to help others in her name."

I stare at him as he speaks, noting how much he looks like Caleb, Gabriel and Asher. It's obvious that they all come from the same gene pool. It's not just the familiarity of his smile that I recognize but it's the strength in his brow and the shape of his nose.

"Corteck is donating some software for us tonight. You're a part of that, aren't you?"

I quickly scan the room for Caleb. I want to be able to introduce myself as his girlfriend although we've never established that's who I am to him. My eyes roll past Ben's head to a clock on the wall of the hotel's dining room. He's late. He told me he'd meet me here at six. It's almost seven and there's no sign of him.

"My boss, Clive Parker, is here to make the presentation. He said you're friends with his wife."

"Lilly." There's a lilt in his voice as he says her name. "We're close friends. You know her, don't you?"

I nod absentmindedly. "I should check in with Clive to make sure everything is set. You'll excuse me?"

"Of course," he says politely.

I look up into his face before I walk away. He's handsome in a way that is different than Caleb. He's more refined and polished. He's kind and as his eyes wander back to his wife, I watch the brilliant smile that consumes her face at the sight of him. That's what I want with Caleb. It's exactly what I've always wanted.

* * *

"Rowan, has Caleb talked to you about the new lingerie boutiques we're opening?"

This is it. This is the pitch I knew was coming.

"Lingerie?" Noah Foster appears next to where Gabriel and I are standing. "My wife told me about this. You're opening lingerie stores now, Gabriel?"

I highly doubt that Noah Foster remembers the brief conversation I had with him years ago at one of his photography shows. At that time, he was selling his pieces for a steep price and women were lining up to be one of his models.

I don't know anyone who posed for him, but I had heard the rumors. There was a contract and the rules were strict. No clothing allowed at all when he had his camera out and that worked both ways. Apparently he worked in the nude.

He smiles down at me and I instantly notice the scar that is now a permanent part of his cheek. I'd asked Asher about it after I met Noah the first time. He'd been stabbed and although he had the resources to seek the most skilled plastic surgeon in the world, he had made a conscious decision to not have his face repaired. It doesn't impact how attractive he is at all. He's hot and when I met him years ago, I made certain to tell Gabriel and Caleb how incredibly handsome I thought Noah was. They'd teased me about it on and off for years.

"You're Rowan Bell, aren't you?" Noah waves his finger in front of my nose. "You and I spoke a number of years ago. I think it was at a gallery."

No way. There's no way he can remember that.

"We did," I say suspiciously. I'm not memorable. It's not that I view myself as not being special; it's more that I'm realistic. He has to meet dozens of people on any given day. It's hard for me to imagine that he'd be impacted enough by our brief conversation that he'd remember me. "How can you possibly remember that?"

"You're Caleb's friend." He glances briefly at Gabriel. "He told me all about you a few weeks after that show and I recognized the name."

"Caleb talked about me?" I shouldn't sound as shocked as I do. I entered the doors of this event as a sophisticated, representative of Cortek. I now sound like a giddy school girl who just realized the boy who sits next to her in Algebra class likes her.

"No," he says quickly with a glint in his eyes. "Caleb talks about you. Every time I see him he talks about you. Rowan graduated with honors. Rowan got a promotion. Rowan is beautiful. It's all Rowan, all the time."

I look up and past his face to quiet my heart. "Caleb and I have been friends for a long time."

"Since you were born." Noah taps my shoulder. "I may know more about you than your own mother does."

I blush at the suggestion. "I had no idea."

He touches my forearm. "My cousin may be mildly obsessed with you. I'd keep an eye on him, if I were you."

I nod as I hear Gabriel's voice interject. "I was just about to offer Rowan a job with the new lingerie division. We should talk about us contracting you to take the photographs for the website and catalogues, Noah."

I know Noah responds, but I can't make out anything he says. The only thing I can focus on is Caleb's smiling face across the room.

FIFTY

"I just want to kiss you once." He brushes his soft, lush lips over mine. "You're wearing one of our dresses."

I pull back to look at him closely. The sight of him in a tuxedo takes my breath away. "I wanted you to see me in one. I don't normally wear your clothes."

"Just my stolen sweatshirts." His voice tightens. "I'm sorry I'm late. I had something I needed to take care of before I got here. "

I want to ask what it is but I know that if it concerned us he'd tell me. I don't want to worry over every small thing that pops up in his life. He made a promise to me that we'd take care of one another and I'm choosing to believe that he'll honor that.

"We should go back out there," I point towards the now crowded ballroom of the hotel. "Clive is going to make a presentation before dinner and I need to be there to support him."

"I understand," he says brusquely. "I'll let you lead the way."

I study his features for a minute, trying to find some clue about what he's feeling. He hadn't shared more than two words with Asher when he walked right past him on his way towards me when he first arrived. When Gabriel approached him, his hand had darted in the air to silence him.

"You're okay?" I reach up to pull a stray piece of lint from the shoulder of his jacket. "Is there something bothering you?"

"I'm good, Rowan." He leans back, his jaw tightening with the movement. "I was just in a rush to get here."

Nervousness pulls at my muscles and I instantly feel my back tense. "I'll go find Clive now. We'll talk in a few minutes, okay?"

"I'll be at the table." He skims his lips across my cheek in a gesture that mimics a kiss. "You know where you can find me."

* * *

The evening had been magical and perfect save for the fact that Caleb had spent most of it talking in the corner on his cell phone. When it came time to introduce me to Noah's wife, Alexa, he had stood silent waiting for me to offer up a connection that brought me to the ballroom. I'd fallen back on my work with Corteck and she had squealed in delight at both the software contribution and the monetary gift that Clive had given tonight.

Now, we're in the back seat of the car while I stare out the window at the traffic flying past us while he makes yet another call.

"I told you that's not going to work for me." Caleb's hand balls into a firm fist on his thigh. "I didn't approve that and unless it's changed by the time I get to the office tomorrow, people are going to be fired."

It's harsh and in the corporate world that we're both a part of, it's sometimes necessary. I keep my eyes focused on the window, catching Caleb's reflection whenever he leans forward and into my view.

"I want to stay at your apartment tonight." He grabs my hand and pulls it to his lips. "I need to be with you."

"We can stay there," I whisper as I turn to look at him. His jaw is tense and his brow is fraught. "You can stay with me whenever you want."

His eyes fall to the necklace around my neck. "That's beautiful. Where did it come from?"

"My friend, Ivy, made it for me." I twist the thin chain in my fingers. "She's a jewelry designer."

"Ivy Marlow?"

"Yes," I answer excitedly. "You know her?"

He shakes his head from side-to-side. "I've heard of her. Her pieces are beautiful. That one is especially exquisite. Maybe I can buy you something for your birthday from her studio. Or she can design something just for you."

I take comfort in the promise that he's already planning my birthday gift. It's not for another two months. "Anything you get me will be perfect."

"Nothing will ever be as perfect as the gift you've given me." He rests my hand against his lips as he pulls me closer.

I curve the side of my body into his. "I don't remember the last gift I ever gave to you, Caleb."

"You gave yourself to me." He wraps his arms around me. "That's the greatest gift I'll ever receive."

FIFTY-ONE

"Rowan, wake up." I feel the brush of a hand against my shoulder. "Wake up."

I murmur into my pillow as I bury my face deeper beneath the blankets. I'm exhausted. After we'd gotten back to the apartment, Caleb had undressed me slowly before he eaten me until I pushed his mouth away. I was so tender and swollen but when he pulled his muscular body over mine, I'd begged him to fuck me.

He had. It was slow, delicious and achingly tender. He'd kissed me with a promise that I'd never felt before and when we both finally came again, he'd whispered something softly in my ear. The words were so vague that I strained to hear but before I could ask him to repeat it, I'd heard the sound of his breathing slowing. He'd fallen asleep instantly and here, in my room, in my bed; I'd curled my body next to his and had drifted off, wrapped snugly in his arms.

"I need you to wake up." His voice is more persistent now. There's a definite urgency woven into the tone. "Please wake up."

I roll over, my eyes fluttering open slowly. The room is still dark and as I reach to the bedside table to find my phone, something falls onto the floor. I hear the faint sound of it hitting the cork floor boards. "What time is it?"

"I don't know." He fumbles with the small lamp that is next to the bed. The bulb is so dim that the light that does fill the space is muted and calming. "It doesn't matter."

That's easy for him to say. He's the boss where he works. He runs the entire show. I, on the other hand, have to answer to Clive Parker. I know I could wander in hours late and my job would still be secure, but I don't want to take advantage of something I value so much. "I'm tired, Caleb. I need to sleep."

"I love you."

I blink twice. That's not what he said. "What did you say?"

"I love you."

As a friend, Rowan. He forgot that part.

"Caleb." I feel a shiver run through me when he sits next to me. "You know that I love you too."

He turns his head to look down at me. "Do you love me the same way I love you?"

I need to sit up. I have to gain some form of perspective in order to have this conversation. I try to scramble my legs up the bed but I falter. I kick without gaining any traction. He does nothing but sit in place and stare at my face.

"Help me." I reach for his arm for leverage and he bends it. I grab hold of his large bicep and use it to help pull me far enough up the bed that I can finally sit and look at him.

He brushes his hand over my forehead. "You're more beautiful every time I see you."

I push the hairs that have stuck to the side of my face when I was sleeping aside. "I'm must be a mess. I was fast asleep."

"I should have told Asher to bring you to quad that day." He presses his lips to my forehead. "I knew it then. I knew Tom was all wrong for you."

I don't mind being woken from a deep sleep if an actual emergency exists. Talking about a man I don't think about anymore, doesn't qualify as important enough to warrant any extra attention. "I don't want to talk about him. That's been over for so long."

"I bought you something." He pushes his bare ass off the bed and leans down to pick up something from the floor. "I wanted to give it to you that day during your senior year."

I dip my chin down to try and get a glimpse of what's hidden within his fist, but I don't see a thing. "What is it?"

He uses his free hand to pull on my arm, motioning for me to sit in his lap. I do. I crawl into it, nuzzling my face into his neck.

"I wasted most of my life, Bell." His chest heaves as he works to catch his breath. "I kept thinking that I had to give up my love for you to have you as my friend."

I look up into his face. "We can be both."

"I was terrified when you loved Tom." He traces a path across my shoulder with his fingers. "I thought we'd never have a chance."

"We have a chance now."

"For so long I've believed that I needed to stay out of the way so you could find a man who would love you the way you deserved to be loved." He rests his chin against my cheek. "I didn't think you wanted me the same way I wanted you."

"I know." I sweep my fingers over his brow. "I know that you didn't think tha"Do you remember when you were a teenager and you had that crush on Ian?"

I laugh into his cheek. "I never had a crush on Ian."

"You did." He pulls me closer to him. "I wanted to kill him. I was so fucking jealous. I saw the way you looked at him and I wanted you to look at me like that."

I breathe in the scent of his skin. "I did look at you like that. I've always looked at you like that."

"When you left the house a few weeks ago," he begins before he stops to kiss my cheek. "When you left the Hamptons house I ran into that bastard."

I tap him playfully on the shoulder. "He's not a bastard."

"He told me he saw you drinking wine in the garden," he whispers into the stillness of the room. "He told me that I was a fool for not telling you how I felt."

"You told me now."

"I don't want to mess this up, Bell." His lips trail over my chin. "I won't mess this up.

I can't live without you now. I won't be able to breathe if we're not us anymore."

I cradle his cheek in my hand as I stare into his eyes. "We won't mess this up. I can't live without you either."

FIFTY-TWO

"Open it."

I stare down at the small circular box he's placed on my bare thigh.

"I want you to open it. I've had it in my apartment all these years."

"You had this in your apartment?" I push at the edge of it.

He nods." That's why I was so late tonight. I had to find it. Once I did I just sat with it. It brought back so many memories."

"What do you mean?" I ask as much to understand as to bide time so I can catch my breath.

"Just open it, Bell. I've been waiting to give it to you for so long."

"You were going to give this to me that day? During semester break?" I can't take my eyes off of the box.

"I bought this to give to you a very long time ago." He edges the box forward with his thumb. "I hoped that one day I could give it to you."

I hesitate before I reach down to touch it. "What is it?"

He swallows hard before he covers my hand with his. "It's something you wanted. You showed it to Asher at that antique shop in South Hampton. My mom took us to the restaurant next door to it for lunch every Thursday and each time, you and Asher would go in the shop to look at it."

I pull my hands to my stomach. "Caleb. No."

"I drove Asher back to the shop one Friday afternoon and he showed it to me." He cups my chin in his hand so our eyes meet. "I bought it on the spot. I've had it since that day."

I know what it is. I already know what it is, but I tentatively pick up the box and carefully open the lid. It's there, just as I remember it. A small silver ring set with one pink pearl. "I remember this."

"You couldn't take your eyes off of it and you couldn't afford to buy it."

"It was really expensive." I try to recall the price and since I was only fourteen or fifteen at the time, I can't.

"It was eighty nine dollars," he says softly. "I bought it, put it in my pocket and when I got back to the house I thought about giving it to you, but the timing wasn't right."

"It wasn't?"

"I was twenty then, Bell."

"I wasn't." I smile.

"It's your ring now." He pulls it gently from the box. "It's a promise that I'll protect you. It's a sign of my need to love you and it's a symbol of everything we mean to each other."

"I love it." I slip it on the ring finger of my right hand. "I'll wear it here for now."

"You'll wear it on whatever finger you want." He pulls my left hand into his and brings it to his lips. "This finger here is reserved for me too."

I kiss his lips knowing that it's a promise that we're making today but it's a reality that has existed between the two of us for the past twenty-five years.

FIFTY-THREE
TWO MONTHS LATER

"I seriously can't believe you're doing this." Caleb pushes the paper on his desk back towards me. "You're going to turn that down."

I glance at the number he's written down again. "I'm not interested."

"I've told you what a fucked up mess Loire is right now, right?" He rakes his hand through his hair. "Gabriel can't get a handle on it and Asher left for San Francisco this morning?"

"He left?" I pretend I hear nothing but that. "Was he excited to go?"

He growls as he turns the paper around and scribbles down another number. "What about this? This has to be enough."

"Nope." I lean back in the chair and cross my legs. "You would get a lot more done if you worked in your actual office instead of here."

"Until an hour ago I was fucking my girlfriend in the bedroom down the hall." He points the pen in the direction of the hallway. "The woman is completely insatiable. She can't get enough of me."

I don't look up from my smartphone. "You must have a really big dick."

"Fuck." His hand hits the desk with a thud. "You didn't just say that my dick is really big, did you?"

"You have a big cock, Caleb." I glance up from my phone. "I've caught you staring at it. You know how big it is."

He shifts slightly in his chair. He has an erection. I can tell by the way he's fidgeting. "I lost my train of thought."

"You were telling me that Asher left for San Francisco." I tap out a quick text message to Clive telling him I'll be in the office within the hour. "That means that he took that job at the recording studio there."

There's a long pause and I wonder if he's about to stand up and bend me over the desk. "I'm going to miss him. We've gotten close the last few months."

It's been two months since Asher came back. He'd been in therapy and for some of the sessions his brothers had gone with him. They'd worked through a lot of his issues as a cohesive unit and when he told them he wanted to move to the west coast to experiment with a career in the music industry, they had both been on board.

"I'm glad he went." I finally look up at him. "I'm proud of you for being so supportive of his dreams."

A ghost of a grin pulls at his lush lips. "I was only supportive because you told me you were coming to work for me. I thought you'd take his place."

"I never said I'd work for you, Caleb. I work for Clive. We've been over this more than a dozen times now."

He leans back in his chair his arms stretching above his head. "You said you would work for me last night."

"When you were eating me out?" I snap back playfully. "Newsflash Foster, when you have your head buried between my legs, I'll say just about anything."

"I'll remember that Bell," he counters. "We need someone brilliant to head up the operations for Loire. They're lingerie boutiques. It's ideal for you."

He may think that all of his pleading is falling on deaf ears, but it's not. I've been resistant to the idea of working with Caleb because I don't want to add any unnecessary strain to our relationship. I love the dynamic we have now. I spend most of my nights here with him and during the day he'll often stop by my office just to tell me how much he loves me. I ache when I'm away from him and since he's started sharing some of his ideas for the Loire division, I've noticed areas that need improvement.

More than any of that, I've run the idea past Clive. He reiterated what he told me about wishing Lilly worked for him. He told me he doesn't want to lose me, but he recognizes the value I can bring to the Foster organization. He also sees how much I love Caleb.

"Is that as high as you're willing to go?" I push the paper back at him.

In short order, he's turned it around and written a new number. It's more than five times what I make now. It's more generous than he needs to be and there's no way I'd accept it as is. "We're getting closer."

"Closer?" He spins it back around and studies the paper. "If I keep adding to this, you're going to make more money than me."

"How is that a problem?" I counter with a smile. "I'm worth it. You know that I am."

He crosses his legs. "If you're teasing me, Bell, you need to stop now. If you're not, I want to know point blank what it's going to take to get you to take over Loire for us."

I run my index finger over my nose. I motion for him to hand me the pen. "Give that to me."

He smiles at the tone of my voice. "Write down your bottom line, Rowan and I'll tell you if we can do it."

I stare at the paper knowing that what I'm about to ask for will change the dynamic between not only Caleb and I, but me and Gabriel, and even Asher too.

I hold the pen above the paper and just before I start to write I look across the desk and into his eyes. "I love you, Caleb. I really love you."

"You'll never love me as much as I love you. Never."

It's the same thing he says every single time I say those words to me. It's what I want to hear each day until I die. I want to hold his hand, and kiss his lips and make love to him for the rest of my life. I write quickly, knowing that his eyes are focused on the paper.

I look at him before I slowly turn it around.

His eyes glide over the paper, then my face and then back to the paper. "You want this?"

"Yes," I say confidentially. "I want that for a salary."

"That's much less than what I just offered to you." He underlines the number with the pen.

"I know." I shuffle closer to the edge of the chair." That's not all I want though."

He leans forward so his elbows are resting on either side of the paper. "You want a percentage of Loire? You want us to give you a stake in that division?"

There's a definite shift in the air between us. "It's a reasonable amount and it will push me to make the business a success."

He looks to the right before his eyes settle back on my face. "You've been thinking about this? You didn't just pull this number from thin air."

"No." I tap the toe of my shoe against his desk. "It's what I want. If you want me to oversee operations for Loire, you're going to need to give me a twenty percent stake in that division."

"You drive a hard bargain." He cocks a brow. "You'll be working with Gabriel. Not me. You know that, right?"

"I know that. I've already talked to your brother about it."

"Why am I not surprised?" He throws his head back in laughter. "Has he already approved this?"

"Verbally." My mouth curves into a smile. "I spoke to him when you were in the shower."

"You know that you're making every one of my dreams come true." He stands quickly and rounds the desk until he's right in front of me.

I reach up with my hands and he gently grabs them pulling me to my feet. "We're going to make new dreams together. I'm where I belong. This is the place I was always supposed to be."

EPILOGUE
SIX MONTHS LATER

"Do you think we can find some time next weekend to have dinner with Graham and his boyfriend?" I look back at where Caleb's resting on the bed behind me. "I feel like I've been neglecting him lately."

"You have been." He pulls on the bottom of my ponytail. "Lingerie has become your life."

I close my tablet before I roll over onto my back. "I want Loire to be a success. I want that for us and for our children."

"Speaking of children," he begins before he takes my left hand in his. "You know that I'm willing to get you an actual engagement ring, right? When I proposed last month, that wasn't the way I envisioned it."

"We were sitting in the garden at the house in the Hamptons. You turned to me and asked me to be your wife. How could it have been more perfect than that?"

"I could have planned it. I have planned it. I wanted to do it on my birthday in Central Park. I was going to get a diamond and drop to one of my knees and…"

"See." I rest my chin on his bare chest. "That wouldn't have meant as much to me."

He peers down his nose in skepticism. "You're telling me that my asking you to marry me on some random Sunday afternoon in a garden is exactly what you wanted?"

I reach forward to brush my lips over his. "I'm telling you that it was perfect and this is the perfect ring."

"Bell." He grazes his fingers over my cheek. "That is an eighty-nine dollar ring I bought at a vintage store a decade ago. It's not the perfect ring."

I rest my head on his chest as I dart my hand into the air above us. "Look at it, Caleb. Just look at it."

I feel him shift beneath me. "It's so small. There's no diamond."

"This ring is every year you loved me. It's every time you ever said my name." I push my cheek into his skin. "It is all about a love that started so long ago that neither of us can remember exactly when."

He strokes my hair. "I don't think I can find another ring that holds that much meaning."

"I know you can't." I lower my hand as I twist around to face him. "This is the only ring I ever want."

"We'll set a wedding date tomorrow?"

"Before we go to work, we'll set a date." I rub my finger over his bottom lip. "I'm going to be Mrs. Foster soon."

"I'll still call you Bell."

"Promise me you'll always call me that." I slide forward to kiss his chin. "I love when you call me that."

"Promise me you'll love me forever and I'll do whatever you want."

"I've loved you forever, Caleb. That will never change."

I close my eyes as I feel his mouth claim mine and I know that every tomorrow I'm going to have will begin in the arms of this man.

PREVIEW OF
HAZE

FEATURING GABRIEL FOSTER

"How long have you worked here?" His voice is cultured, deep and smooth. It's not uncommon to hear a voice like that in this boutique. I've worked here for six weeks now and at least twice a week a man with too much money and an insatiable need to see young women dressed in expensive lingerie will come waltzing through the doors.

"Welcome to Liore," I say softly as I glance to my left to where he's standing.

I have to look up. He's large, not just in height but in his shoulder's breadth. His eyes are a rich brown, his hair just as dark. His nose is sculptured and his jaw has a definite curve to it. The suit he's wearing is dark blue, perhaps even black. It's hard to tell under the chandelier lights that decorate this opulent space.

"Isla." His eyes fly over my chest before they settle on my nametag. "It's nice to meet you, Isla."

"It's lovely to meet you…" I pause. It's not only because I've been instructed to grab the name of every customer to give them a personal shopping experience. I want to know his name.

"Gabriel," he offers with a light touch of his hand on mine.

The name is oddly familiar as I work to place it, I see him peering across the boutique at my boss. "Is there something I can help you find, Gabriel? Are you purchasing something for a girlfriend, or perhaps, your wife?"

His expression shifts slightly. "I have neither."

That's a pity but it's not. This is exactly the type of man I envisioned in my mind's eye when I arrived in Manhattan. I graduated from high school less than two years ago and my dreams of attending Julliard on a scholarship had vanished as quickly as my clean record when I broke one too many rules in high school.

"Is there something in particular that you're looking for?" I catch the faint wave of the hand of one of my co-workers across the aisle. I ignore it because when a customer is ready to buy, the store could be engulfed in flames, and I'm not moving an inch. The commissions here are the highest I've ever earned in retail and the secret to guarantee a big sale is to make the customer feel as though they're the only one in the boutique.

His eyes scan the various bras we have displayed before they move to the lace panties and garters. "If I asked you to try something on for me, Isla, would you do that? Would you take me into one of the change rooms with you?"

I've read the employee handbook. No, I skimmed it briefly while on my way to work that first day weeks ago. The number one rule is to never take a customer into the rooms. Men who lead you into those quiet spaces are craving more than a private fashion show. I know that. "I'm sorry, Gabriel. That's against company policy."

He studies my face carefully. The dark shadow around my blue eyes looks hideous in the alarming bright light of the morning, but in here it's sensual and alluring. My shoulder length blonde hair is straight today, a sharp contrast to my high cheekbones. I'm here to sell lingerie and the light pink wrap around dress I'm wearing accentuates everything it needs to. He hasn't walked away yet, so he's still primed to buy.

He closes the short distance between us as he steps towards me. "You don't strike me as the type of young woman who follows all the rules."

It's tempting. Not just because of the extra money I'd find in my pocket. "I don't follow rules, Gabriel. If you want a private show, I can come to your office after work."

His brow cocks with the suggestion. "Is that something you offer to customers often, Isla?"

I've never offered it before. "I only offer it to the ones who peak my interest."

"I'll give you my card." His hand dips into the inner pocket of his suit jacket.

I take it from his long, elegant fingers and look down at it. I don't have time to read the details before my boss is upon us.

I turn to look at her but she's staring at Gabriel. Her hand leaps to his shoulder.

"Mr. Foster," she says slowly. "I see that you've met our newest girl. Isla, you're explaining everything we offer to Mr. Foster, yes?"

I look down at the card of Mr. Gabriel Foster, the CEO of Foster Enterprises and the man who owns this boutique.

"Isla has been very cordial." He reaches to brush his hand over my forearm. "She's coming by my office today. I'll expect you at four, Isla."

"At four," I repeat back. "I'll be there at four, Sir."

His eyes skim slowly over my body before they stop on my face. "Don't be late and bring those samples we spoke of."

I freeze as his hand runs up my arm before he brushes past me towards the front of the shop.

PREVIEW OF
EMBER

A THREE PART SERIES

"If you're coming back to my place I need to buy some condoms."

The fork in my hand stops in mid-air. I don't look up. I can't. I've barely taken one bite of the roasted squash salad the waiter brought me not more than four minutes ago. This is New York City. This is the place where I thought I'd find the love of my life. What the hell was I thinking?

"You're up for coming back, right?"

My head darts up and I study him. This might actually be the first time I've seriously looked right at him. I'm on a blind date. Maybe the term itself holds more meaning than the literal. Obviously, I had no idea what Larry looked like before I walked through the doors of Axel NY a half hour ago. More than that,

I couldn't have predicted that we'd be talking about sex before I'd finished my first glass of wine.

"I don't know you," I say bluntly. "Why would I go home with you?"

It's a question that borders heavily on rhetorical. I don't think that Larry's bright enough to weave those tangled pieces of subtly together. He's an assistant to a paralegal. That says a lot about his drive in life considering he looks like he's in his mid-forties. He's also dying to be fucked. He's not shy about it at all.

"We're on a date, Bridget…" The words linger there on his thin, smug lips. He doesn't add to them because why would he? Those words have clearly and succinctly spelled out every intention that he has. They aren't masked in anything but the truth. Larry wants his dick to see some action tonight and I'm apparently the main attraction in that circus.

"It's just a date," I explain. "I'd like to get to know you first."

"Why?" He pushes the food from his fork into his mouth and chews.

"I'm not interested in a quick fuck."

His unruly brow cocks. "I heard you were up for just about anything."

Fuck you, Zoe Beck. Fuck you for whatever the hell you said to him when you arranged this date.

"I have no idea what my friend told you about me," I pause while I contemplate how to put this delicately. I stare at him. The wayward piece of kale that is stuck between his front teeth is only adding to the allure that is Larry.

He leans forward on the table. The patch on the elbow of his inexpensive suit jacket brushes against the linen tablecloth. "This place isn't cheap. I brought you here because I thought you were a sure thing."

A sure thing? A fucking sure thing?

I wince at the words. "The only sure thing tonight is that you're going home alone."

It's obvious immediately that Larry is contemplating those words with all the grace of a pack of wild dogs. His hand slams heavily against the spotless white linen tablecloth. "I didn't buy you that expensive salad for nothing. The least you can do is bloNo, the least I can do is tell him to fuck right off. "I am not interested in you."

"I'm not interested in you either." He flings his napkin at me and it lands squarely in my squash salad. I was actually going to have another bite of that. "I like brunettes."

Touché. "I like men with hair."

Ouch. I can feel Larry's pain from across the table. Obviously no one, including all the brunettes he's been with, has pointed out the bad comb over that's happening on the top of his odd shaped head.

'We're leaving now."

I actually look to the right and the left to see who Larry is talking to. I'm gathering that he's still engaged in a conversation with me even though I'm trying desperately to ignore him. People are starting to stare and I have no aversion to a little extra attention, but tonight, I don't want to be the main attraction in Larry's sideshow.

"Get up." He grabs tightly to my bare bicep and yanks hard.

I cry out sharply. Considering the fact that most of my body is still stuck next to this table in a chair my arm can't leave with Larry. "Let go of me."

"Is there a problem?" A deep, husky voice asks.

I turn towards it even though Larry is still trying to separate my arm from my shoulder to take as a consolation prize. I look up into the dark eyes of a brown haired man. He's staring down at me with a noticeable look of concern on his face.

"Hey," he calls across the table at Larry. "Enough. You're hurting her."

"Get lost." Larry loosens his grip only momentarily. "My girlfriend and I don't need your help."

Wait. No. Hell no.

'I'm not your girlfriend," I growl at him. "Let go of my arm already."

"You're coming with me." Larry pulls harder and I can't help but cry out in pain. Within an instant my arm is free and the lapel of Larry's jacket is firmly entrenched in the fisted hands of the handsome man with the dark eyes.

"Are you okay?" He cocks a winged brow. "Did he hurt you?"

"I'm fine." My voice is quiet and small. Maybe I'm not as fine as I thought. I lean my hands on the table, suddenly feeling dizzy.

I hear movement behind me before I sense someone crouching next to me. "He's gone. Are you sure you're okay?"

I turn to the left and look into the same deep brown eyes. "I'm fine. He just shook me up."

"He may have torn something in your shoulder." He presses it lightly with his fingers. "I'd get it checked out if it's sore tomorrow."

"Are you a doctor?" I know he's probably on a date with someone. The dark suit he's wearing doesn't hide his muscular frame.

"No." A small grin pulls at the corner of his mouth. "I'm a firefighter. I'm Dane."

"Bridget," I say with a wince as I try to move my arm to shake his hand.

"I'm taking you to the ER now." He pulls on the back of my chair. "Come with me."

I don't protest. Why would I? He's a fireman and he wants to rescue me. I may actually have to thank Zoe for this date, after all.

THANK YOU!

Thank you for purchasing and downloading my book. I can't even begin to put to words what it means to me. If you enjoyed it, please remember to write a review for it. Let me know your thoughts! I want to keep my readers happy.

For more information on upcoming series as well as updates, please visit my website, www.deborahbladon.com. There are book trailers and other goodies to check out.

If you want to chat with me personally, please LIKE my page on Facebook. I love connecting with all of my readers because without you, none of this would be possible.

www.facebook.com/authordeborahbladon
Thank you, for everything.

ABOUT THE AUTHOR

Deborah Bladon has never read a romance hero she didn't like. Her love for romance novels began when she was old enough to board the bus, library card in hand to check out the newest Harlequin paperbacks. She's a Canadian by heart, and by passport, but you can often spot her in New York City sipping a latte and looking for inspiration for her next story. Manhattan is definitely her second home.

She cherishes her family and believes that each day is a gift for writing, for reading, and for loving.

Printed in Great Br
by Amazon